Half an Inch of Water

Also by Percival Everett

Half an Inch of Water

Stories

PERCIVAL EVERETT

Graywolf Press

"Finding Billy White Feather" first appeared in the *Virginia Quarterly Review*
"Graham Greene" first appeared in *Callaloo*
"Little Faith" first appeared in the *Literary Review*
"Stonefly" first appeared in *Denver Quarterly*

This publication is made possible, in part, by the voters of Minnesota through a Minnesota State Arts Board Operating Support grant, thanks to a legislative appropriation from the arts and cultural heritage fund, and through a grant from the Wells Fargo Foundation Minnesota. Significant support has also been provided by Target, the McKnight Foundation, Amazon.com, and other generous contributions from foundations, corporations, and individuals. To these organizations and individuals we offer our heartfelt thanks.

Published by Graywolf Press
212 Third Avenue North, Suite 485
Minneapolis, Minnesota 55401

www.graywolfpress.org

Published in the United States of America

ISBN 978-1-55597-719-1

4 6 8 9 7 5 3

Library of Congress Control Number: 2015939973

Cover design: Kapo Ng

For Dorothy and Leo

Contents

Half an Inch of Water

Little Faith

1

A spring-fed creek ran through the ranch and so even in the harshest summer weeks there was a narrow lane of willows and green grass. Moose and elk browsed and left deep tracks in the muddy banks. Sam Innis had grown up there with his mother, his father having died in the war in Vietnam. The woman had clung to her husband's dream, leasing out pasture, raising a few beefs, and giving piano lessons to the ranch children in the valley. She turned down many offers on the place, saying that even imagining such a thing would be a betrayal. Love of the spread had been rubbed into him like so much salve, a barrier against whatever was out there in the world, a layer of peace. His mother held him close, not wanting to lose her only remaining family, but let the ranch, the land, shape him. She let him go for his education and died while he was away at vet school. He had the old woman cremated and her ashes were mixed now into the dusty furrows, mud, and deep tracks of life of that place. At dusk, when the owls and bats were whispering about, Sam would sit by the creek and watch the few trout rise to some hatch.

The desert rolled like always, constant, brown, ocher, and especially red in the distance. The pressure of people, the efforts of people had killed off much of the life, but none of the desert. His mother had said it: you can kill everything, you can tear it all up and build, you can pipe water to it, but the desert is the desert, more desert every day. It unfolded itself before him as he crested the ridge and started down the big curve of highway that would take him to the road to his place. The late-morning sun was still behind him, but the shadows of the sage were beginning to shorten.

Sam and his wife were driving home from a memorial service. The oldest resident of the reservation had died at ninety-two. That was old for anyone, but especially for a Native man. Someone had told Sam that the life expectancy of an Indian male was forty-four. The Indian man who offered the statistic did so without the slightest show of bitterness or even fear. It's just a thing, he said. The service had been at the Episcopal church. Sam didn't like churches.

Sam didn't know what the old man's death had been like. Apparently he was walking one minute and not the next. Sam hadn't known Old Dave Wednesday very well, for only a few years, but once, while Sam was out examining the horses at the tribal ranch, the two sat together on a hillside.

I am an old man, Dave said.

I suppose, Sam agreed. How old are you exactly?

Ninety.

That's old. My mother didn't live to be that old.

They had hiked up the hill to look down at the ranch. Dave was telling him how the tribe planned to bring water down-mountain via an old-fashioned drainage ditch.

Dave pointed at the hills with an open, shaky hand. From over there. Them surveyors came and looked and said it was possible. Said we need some engineers. And all of them want to get paid.

Sam nodded.

Dave rubbed his knees. I'm glad to be sitting. I can't walk like I used to.

None of us can, Sam said.

I will die soon.

Sam was not so comfortable with this talk, but he said, We all die. He hated this platitude.

So I'm told. And there is nothing wrong with it. If you do it right, then you don't have to do it again.

They sat silent for a bit. Sam looked at the horses in the pasture below and then over at the hills where the water would come from. Measure twice, cut once, he said.

Dave laughed. Then he laughed again, at something else.

What is it? Sam asked.

Us, the old man said. We are Sam and Dave. We are soul men. He laughed again, louder.

Sam brought the pickup to a stop on the gravel next to the house. He and Sophie sat there for a few seconds and let the ticking of the killed engine settle into silence. They stared ahead at the fenced pasture and the willows far off along the creek. A colt pranced around his mother.

You okay? Sophie asked.

Sam looked at her.

About having been in a church.

Sam chuckled. Yes, I'm okay. Let's get changed so we can take care of these beasts.

Zip, the border collie, greeted them at the door and followed them into the house through the kitchen. Sophie stopped at the counter to check the phone messages. Sam walked upstairs, peeled off his jacket, and undid the knot of his tie. He sat on the bed and kicked off his shoes.

These shoes hurt my feet, he said as Sophie entered.

You always say that.

It's always true. You should bury me in them. That way you'll know I won't be doing any ghostly walking.

I was looking forward to your ghostly walking.

You are a sweet-talker, aren't you?

Yes, I am. She unhooked the back of her dress and let it slide down her body to the floor.

All right. And you're a tease.

Yes, I am.

Come here, Missy. He reached for her hand.

You know I love when you talk cowboy.

Do you now? Come here.

Me?

Yes, you, ma'am.

He stood and held her, kissed her.

The house shifted, it seemed. Then the whole structure shook, swayed as if riding a wave. They clung to each other. There was a crash downstairs. The clock bounced off Sam's nightstand. And it was over and everything was quiet for a brief moment and then the mules were braying and the horses were calling out. Then Zip started barking.

Wow. Sophie dropped to a knee and comforted the dog. Earthquake?

I'm guessing so.

Sam slipped back into his dress shoes and headed for the stairs. Sophie grabbed her robe and pulled it on. She followed him down. Sam wondered if there would be another tremor. At the bottom he could see that the framed picture of his mother had fallen, but only the glass had cracked. Other pictures were askew, but nothing seemed to be broken. They stepped into the mudroom and changed into their boots, then walked out the kitchen door. The world didn't appear any different. The sky was cloudless. The hills were still standing in the distance. Zip ran in circles. The horses were stirred up. The skittish mare was kicking her stall wall in the near barn. A loose barn door that Sam had been meaning to repair for weeks now lay flat in the dust.

You go settle the horses, Sam said. I'll check the propane.

Sam watched Sophie move off. She stopped to say something soft to the little donkey in the paddock just outside the barn. Zip stayed with Sam. She always stayed with Sam. He went to the cabinet on the exterior wall next to the back door and grabbed a pipe wrench and a spray bottle filled with soapy water. The large green propane tank was thirty yards from the house. It looked fine. He listened as he looked at the gauge and felt around the joins. He sprayed the connections and saw no bubbles. The line to the house was underground; there was no checking that. He walked back to the house and into the kitchen. He pushed the stove away from the wall and bit and sprayed the line, all good. In the cellar he checked the furnace. The pilot was surprisingly still lit. No leaks. Same with the water heater. Sophie was in the kitchen when he came back up.

Everything all right? she asked.

All good.

I can't believe we had an earthquake. She sat at the table. I didn't even know we had a fault.

You don't, Sam said.

Who's the sweet-talker?

The barns?

Just that door. Horses are scared.

Horses are always scared. They'll be fine in ten minutes. Sam set the spray bottle on the table. I guess we should turn on the radio.

They sat in the kitchen, drank tea, and listened to the local station. There had been a quake, the magnitude of which had not been determined, a surprise to everyone and a source of incessant chatter. There was little to report in the way of damage and they quickly grew tired of people calling in to repeat the experience of the previous caller. Broken canned goods, cracked washer drums, ruined china sets. One woman called to say that in the minutes right before the quake her chickens, to a hen, had laid an egg.

And how does she know that? Sophie, said laughing.

The rooster told her, Sam said. He looked out the window. I figure the office phone will start ringing soon. Now that everybody has figured out they're all right, they'll start seeing stuff wrong with their animals.

The phone rang.

Sam picked up.

It was Terry Busch from north of town. She was a new transplant, from California to live the quiet life. I want to buy a horse and I need a vet check, she said.

What'd you think of the quake? Sam asked.

That was hardly a quake, the woman said.

I guess not for you.

There's this beautiful leopard Appaloosa down near Randy Gap. Can you meet there this afternoon? Two?

Sam looked at the clock. It was twelve thirty. Two thirty?

That's good.

I'll meet you at the flashing light at two thirty.

He hung up.

Didn't sound like an emergency, Sophie said.

City woman wants a horse, Sam said. Everybody ought to have a horse. And the lucky ones of us can have mules.

You and your mules.

I'm supposed to look at Watson's mare at one. That won't take long and that's on the way to the Gap.

What about lunch?

I'll take an apple with me.

Sophie made a disapproving face.

Two apples.

Just make sure you don't feed one to a horse.

Yes ma'am.

Sam walked out of the house and to his work truck, where he in-spected his vet pack. It was his habit. He restocked every time he returned home and always checked his supplies before setting out. The sky remained clear, if a little cool, but heat was on the way. Zip hopped into the truck before him.

He drove the unused back roads to the ranch of Wes Watson. The back way was actually faster, but rough on the suspension, the truck's and his. He looked at Zip as they bounced along. Probably not the best thing for my prostate, he said to her. The mare he was seeing he'd seen before for vaccinations and once for a hoof problem. Now Wes wanted to breed her.

Wes met him at his truck. Greetings.

Greetings to you, Sam said, laughing.

I thought it seemed like a pleasant way to, to—

Greet someone? Sam offered.

More or less.

So, you want to breed the Paint. She in season?

You're here to tell me.

Going to use live cover?

Nope. Sperm's on the way.

Sam nodded. He followed Wes into the barn. The quarter horse was standing calmly, already cross-tied in a washstand and backed up against a rail. Sam looked at her while he pulled on his glove. Well, her tail's up, isn't it?

Her tail's always up, Wes said.

Sam gave the horse's neck a stroke and moved down to her flank. He inserted his gloved hand into the animal's vagina. She took a step but stayed calm. He could see she was in estrus before he was inside. He felt around, shook his head.

What is it? Wes asked.

We might have a problem, Sam said. He felt around more. I think she's got a hematoma.

Is that bad?

Sam slowly removed his arm and hand. No, not bad. But she won't be getting knocked up for a while. She's going to have to cycle a few times before this resolves itself. Won't affect her fertility. We'll keep an eye on her.

How do you know it's not a tumor?

The other ovary feels normal. If it were a tumor, the other would probably be smaller than normal. Plus, she's not acting all crazy with hormones. I'm going to take some blood to be sure.

All right. That's disappointing.

Sam flexed his hand, rolled down his shirtsleeve. She sure is a pretty horse, I'll give you that. I see why you want to breed her.

She's a looker. Even tempered, too.

They walked back to Sam's truck. Zip lay in the vehicle's shadow.

So, did you feel the shaker? Wes asked.

Oh yeah.

We hardly did. The wind chimes on the porch shook. That was about it. So, where you headed from here?

Down to Randy Gap. Vet check.

Wes nodded. So, I just leave her alone? Wes asked about the horse.

Leave her alone. Treat her like a horse. Sam opened a cabinet in the pack in the back of his pickup, pulled out a syringe kit and some vials. I'll get me a little bit of blood and I'll be on my way.

You know, you're okay, Wes said.

Sam looked at him. How's that?

You know, being a black vet out here. I have to admit, I had my doubts.

About what exactly?

Whether you'd make it.

You mean fit in?

I guess that's what I mean, yeah.

Wes, I grew up here. Grade school. High school. I've never fit in. I probably will never fit in. I accept that.

Wes's face was now blank. He didn't understand. He was just a degree away from cocking his head like a confused hound.

Sam said, Thanks, Wes. I'm glad you think I'm okay.

That's all I was saying.

I know, Wes.

Randy Gap, eh? Bad medicine down there.

That what folks in the tribe say?

No, that's what I say. You don't have to be no Indian to spot it.

I suppose that's right.

Sam left Wes there in the sun, walked back into the barn to collect blood from the Paint mare.

Randy Gap was the confluence of two draws and two roads and had nothing to do with anyone named Randy or Randolph. It had been so named because supposedly whenever old-timers drove cattle through there the bulls would get crazy horny and slow everything down. Now it was the weather in the gap that slowed everything down; snow and rain and wind seemed to concentrate on the area. It was windy when Sam found Terry Busch waiting there, leaning against her Subaru. He crunched to a halt on the gravel roadside.

Hey, Terry.

Doc.

So, you want to buy yourself a new horse.

It's not far, she said. Couple of miles.

I'll follow you. He watched the woman walk back to her car. She was his age, but she looked younger. Or maybe it was that he looked older. What was forty-four supposed to look like?

He trailed her to a dirt road and then a half mile in to a trailer home surrounded by pipe corrals and paddocks. Horses stood in most of the enclosures, some clean, some not. He'd seen places like this before and there was little good about them. He parked behind Terry and got out. He left Zip in the truck.

A teenage boy came from the trailer. He wore a tight T-shirt that said *One in the Oven* with an downward-pointing arrow. He tossed his cigarette into the dirt.

Well, here I am, Terry said.

I'll get him, the kid said without expression.

Warm, Sam said, referring to the boy's greeting.

The teenager came back with a fifteen-hand Appaloosa gelding with a nicely defined blanket on his rump. The horse was clean and freshly shod.

Isn't he beautiful? Terry was not playing the role of the cool buyer. She stepped back and looked at the horse.

Sam circled the animal. Nice markings, all right, he said. But that's not why I'm here, is it? He reached out to shake the kid's hand. I'm Sam Innis, the vet.

The boy shook his hand. Jake.

Sam let go of the boy's limp mitt. Let's take a look at him. Anything you want to tell us?

The boy shook his head. I don't know anything. They come in, we sell them. This one eats everything we put down, I can tell you that.

You mind trotting him over there about twenty yards and then back to me? Sam watched as the kid led the horse away. They kicked up dust. Sam studied the animal. As they were coming back he said, He's a little wide in the chest. See how he paddles? Like he's swimming.

Is that bad? Terry asked.

Better than being too narrow and knocking his feet together. He won't be much good at jumping anything. He asked the boy to repeat the trot away and back. He's loose in the caboose. Terry, his legs are everywhere. What do you want to do with him?

Ride trails, that's all.

Sam nodded. He might be okay. I can see why you like him. He's pretty. Being wide is a good thing for your comfort. Well, let's take a closer look. He's not exactly wide through the stifles. Sam caught himself. He didn't want to be too negative. After all, Terry liked the horse.

The winded boy came back with the horse and stood quietly. Sam measured the circumference of the leg just below the knee. Good bone. He grabbed the knee. He's just a little buck-kneed.

Terry came close and looked with Sam.

Sam looked at Terry. He's got a beautiful coat. Flies don't seem to bother him. Sam looked at the horse's eyes and then at the boy. Just how much bute did you give him?

A little, the boy admitted, caught off guard.

What is it? Terry asked.

Will he lunge? Sam asked.

Yeah, Jake said.

Sam took the lead rope from the boy and got the horse trotting counterclockwise around him. He stopped him and picked up his left forefoot.

What is it? Terry asked.

They gave the horse a drug for pain. He's got some navicular issues.

I mean, Terry, you can live with all the problems I'm finding, I'm sure. Corrective shoes will help his heels, but he won't be much good for long or strenuous rides. What are they asking for him?

Three grand, Jake said.

Sam smiled. I wouldn't pay more than eight hundred.

You're crazy, the kid said. He was red in the face.

I've been told that, Sam said. Terry, I can keep checking him, but it won't get better.

This horse is sound, the kid snapped.

Sam nodded.

I guess I'll pass, Terry said to Jake.

So that's it? The boy grunted.

Thanks for showing him to me, Terry said.

Yeah, right. He muttered something to himself as he walked the horse away.

Sam walked with Terry back to her car.

I think he's pissed, she said.

He was trying to rip you off. Maybe not the kid, but the guy he works for. Healthy horses are expensive enough to take care of.

Thanks, Doc.

Sam felt bad. Terry had had high hopes for the animal, was a little bit in love with him. He watched her fall in behind the wheel of her car, start it, and have a bit of trouble getting turned around.

Sam climbed into his own truck and laughed when he had the same diffcult time getting himself about-faced. He drove home.

2

Sophie answered the ringing phone as Sam stepped into the kitchen.

We're fine, she said. What about you? That's good. Oh, I see. He just walked in. She handed the phone to Sam. It's the sheriff.

Dale, Sam said.

You okay over there? Any damage? the sheriff asked.

Nothing. What's up?

I'd like you to come out here and give us a hand. We've got a lost little girl next to the reservation. Up in the Creeks.

How long has she been lost?

About six hours. I'm down at the little store at the flashing light. Only place I can get a signal on my damn phone.

Can you get in touch with Eddie over there?

Yes.

Have Eddie get me a horse ready. That way I won't have to waste time getting one loaded into a trailer.

All right, you got it. I've got six men out now, four on horseback, two on foot. Of course the only thing the quake damaged was the helicopter. We're waiting on one to come from Casper. Duncan's flying his Beechcraft around.

Where are you exactly?

You'll see us. Just take the road on through to the far side of the reservation. Just past the dip.

Oh, and Sam.

Yes.

The girl is deaf.

I'm on my way. Be there in less than an hour. He hung up.

Sophie was standing close. What?

Little deaf girl is lost out in the Owl Creeks.

That's got to be Sadie White Feather's girl.

Dale didn't tell me her name.

She's so tiny.

When Sam came back from the washroom, Sophie handed him a pack.

Water, she said. Some fruit and some cookies. The cookies are for the child.

Yes ma'am. I'm going to grab my chaps from the tack shed. Might have to pop some brush.

He gave her a kiss and stepped outside, called for Zip.

The sheriff had set up a staging area at the head of a little-used trail. It was a hundred square miles of barren, desolate, arid hills, full of worthless ore and seasonal creeks that could flood in a blink. The county/reservation line was somewhere around there, but no one knew for sure and no one cared. Sam and Zip got out of the truck and walked to the sheriff. He was trying to talk with someone on a handheld radio. Sadie White Feather was sitting on a metal folding chair a few yards away. She did not look up at the sound of Sam's approach.

Dale, Sam said.

I'm glad you're here. These damn radios work for shit in these hills. I don't know where the fuck anybody is.

Sam looked at the hills. Old Dave Wednesday would never set foot in them, called them haunted. Sam had actually liked the place, had ridden there once.

The tribal police put me in charge. Mainly because I'm supposed to have a helicopter. But I don't. Anyway, the whole tribal force, all three of them, are out there looking.

Okay.

Along with my two deputies and that new ranger, Epps.

What exactly is the situation?

Dale glanced over at Sadie White Feather. He motioned for Sam to follow him away a few paces. Girl's name is Penny. She went and wandered off away from the family's camp and just never came back. She was here with her mother, aunt, uncle, and grandmother. Her uncle's a tribal cop; he's out looking. The aunt and grandma went to find the father.

Sam nodded. They see anybody else around?

No. Did I mention that the radio reception is crappy in these damn hills? Cell phones are worse.

Any sign yet?

Nothing reported.

Sam stepped over to look at the map the sheriff had spread out on the hood of his rig. It was held down from the wind by rocks. Circles had been drawn and Xs were placed in spots.

She's only nine, Sam. How much ground could she have covered?

A lot, Sam said. And these canyons are just crazy. You could pass by the same wash three times and never know it. Mind if I talk to Sadie?

Be my guest.

Zip had already made it over to the woman and pushed up under her hand. Sadie was absently patting the dog's head.

Sadie, Sam said.

The woman looked up.

It's me, Sam Innis. You know my wife, Sophie.

Sadie nodded.

I'm going to go out and help look for Penny. Sam dropped to one knee, faced the direction she faced, and studied the same empty space. But I need to ask you a few questions. You've been asked a bunch, I know, but a couple more, okay? They tell me Penny's nine.

Nine and a half.

Exactly where and when did you last see her?

She was playing over by those yellow mounds. She pointed with an open hand. She was throwing rocks. She glanced over at me and I signed for her to stop throwing rocks, but she pretended not to see and kept on throwing. My sister said to just let her throw rocks, she wasn't hurting nothing. I started cooking. I was making chokecherry gravy. When I looked back over there, I didn't see her. I didn't think anything of it and I went back to cooking. Then I got to thinking about how she can't hear snakes and so I went over and looked for her. I looked all over and then my sister and her husband started looking and we couldn't find her. I guess that was about eight thirty, maybe nine.

Is she completely deaf?

Yes.

Can you show me how to sign her name?

You just put one finger to your forehead and move it out. Like this. It's kind of a joke. We call her "one cent." You know, a penny is one cent.

Like this? Sam repeated the motion.

The woman nodded. She might laugh at you.

How do I say *friend*?

Sadie showed him. Crossed fingers this way and that.

Got it. And that's about all my old head can hold. And is Penny left- or right-handed?

Right. She does some things with her left. She brushes her teeth with her left hand. I've tried and I can't do it.

I know you were making breakfast, but did she eat anything this morning?

Nothing.

Did she drink water?

She always drinks a lot of water. Oh, she had a juice box, too.

Good, that's a good thing. What about her shoes? What kind of shoes is she wearing?

Sneakers, Sadie said. You know, those kind the kids love with the heels that light up. They're a little small on her. I guess that doesn't matter.

It matters, Sam said. Everything matters. Tell me, is Penny a smart girl?

All As. She's very, very smart. She knows the capitals of all the states.

How much does she weigh?

Not much. I don't know. She's little. Fifty pounds? Not even.

Thanks, Sadie. We're going to find her, okay? That was what Sam said, because that's was what one always said in these situations. He'd been a tracker for a long time and he'd never once set out believing he would find anyone.

Sam walked back to the sheriff.

You need an article of clothing for your dog? Dale asked.

She's not a scent dog. She can't smell bacon cooking. But any dog is better than three men.

The roan over there is what Eddie drove over for you. He's driving the highway, just in case. And here's a radio, for all the good it will do you. Just try it periodically. It might work.

Dale's radio awoke with static and he stepped away, trying to find a stronger signal. Sam looked at the map again, then walked over to where Sadie had last seen the child throwing rocks. He picked up a few stones and hurled them at a boulder. Not far from the yellow formation was a narrow wash between waist-high walls. Not so intriguing for an adult, Sam thought, but probably irresistible for a child. The ground there had been pretty well trampled by men's boots and shod horses, and then it became rocky. He decided he'd follow the wash.

He walked back to the roan, gave him a rub on the neck. He knew the horse, had treated him a couple of times. He of course knew the horse did not remember him. He tightened the cinch of the synthetic saddle. The horse was a short, sturdy, big-butted quarter horse, good for breaking through growth. He mounted, whistled for Zip, and rode on.

Into the ravine. The walls were saddle high until they opened up, spread away from the wash as it widened, and joined another drainage. He saw where a couple of riders had gone on north. He veered down and around a steep hill and rode on a mile or so. He checked his radio and already it was useless. These hills were full of something magnetic, he figured, or it was just spirits and Old Dave had been right. He messed with the squelch on the radio and was able to hear Dale swearing at the other end.

He rode on slowly, looking ahead and scouting the distance and casting a glance down to study the ground and brush. He looked for something, anything, the tiniest thing out of the ordinary, a drag, a broken stick, even an animal acting strangely. The ground was baked hard with a fine layer of loose sand that the wind played with. He dismounted and looked closely at the surface, moved his sight up slowly, squinted. He stared and stared. A lopsided creosote bush caught his eye. He led the horse to it. It was broken about a foot off the ground. It was a fairly fresh break. Anything could have caused the damage; he knew that. Still it was something. He combed the ground around and near the bush. Then, in a spot protected from the wind, he thought he saw some transfer of soil over pebbles. Hardly a definite sign, but he decided to view it as transfer and that gave him a direction. He observed the clouds and sky to the east. Back in the saddle, he watched Zip sniff around some coyote scat. She left it in short order and heeled to the roan.

Sam rode up to a bit of high ground and looked over the terrain. He had come to an expanse of flat ground. Far off to the north he could make out a couple of riders. Above him a hawk circled high. There was an outcropping to the east, the direction he'd chosen. There was nothing between him and the rocks and so he rode toward the formation, the light sinking behind him.

The sun was a couple of hours from setting and was already giving the west-facing rocks an eerie bronze shimmer. The wind picked up and blew sand in sheets. There would be no trail, human or otherwise. He stopped and examined a couple of odd spots, thought one might have been where a small person had stopped to rest. He recalled how easy it was for a man to see what he wanted to see.

The outcropping was surprisingly larger than it had seemed from a distance. There was plenty of space between boulders for a person to wander into and get lost. The wind was whipping now and in these rocks it was bouncing and twisting in all directions. The temperature was dropping. He considered letting the horse stand on a dropped rein, but tied up to some sage instead. He tried the radio. Nothing. He looked at the sky for a plane or helicopter. Nothing.

Sam left the horse and with Zip wended his way into the formation. They came out into a bowl, the floor of which was an expanse of flat rock. On the table of rock were a considerable number of rattlesnakes basking in the last rays of the day's sun, trying to collect all the warmth they could from the stone. In the middle of the flat area, in the middle of the snakes, was a washtub-shaped rock and on it sat a little girl. Sam called out and immediately realized the futility in that. He told Zip to stay, said it twice. His actions now were very important. If he startled the child she might panic and move into the snakes. He didn't know if she was aware of the snakes. His back was to the west and so he would be in silhouette. Also, with his back to the west he couldn't use his watch face or anything else to reflect the sun to get the girl's attention. He moved left, moved to put the sun

someplace else. He could see that her eyes were open, but she stared
blankly at the rocks thirty or so feet in front of her. He was losing the
day. It was colder still. He reached down and collected a handful of
pebbles. He repeated his command to Zip to stay. He walked into
the snakes, wishing he were wearing taller boots. His Wellingtons
came up only to midcalf.

He pitched a pebble at the girl. It landed without effect near her
heels. He tossed another and it skittered across the plane of rock in
front of her and she saw it. She turned and looked at Sam. He froze.
Stepping as he was through the snakes, he was certain that his posture, his body language would be difficult for her to read. He must
have looked strange. He could see fear coming over her face. He
put his hands up and signed *friend* to her. Whether he was doing it
correctly, he didn't know. The fact that he was signing at all at least
let her know that he knew something about her. He put his hands
out, palms down, as if to tell her to relax. He then pointed to the
snakes. It was unclear whether she was seeing them for the first
time, but she pulled her feet up onto the rock and held her knees.
Good, Sam said, but didn't know how to sign that, so he nodded.
Perhaps she could read lips and then he wondered how much lip
he showed under his bush of a mustache. He signed *friend* again. He
looked back to see if Zip was obeying his last command and she
was. Penny was wearing only a T-shirt and sweatpants. She was
no doubt feeling the cold or would be soon. A snake rattled near
Sam. He looked around and tried to locate the agitated animal. Zip
barked. Sam again gestured to the child to remain calm. He took
another step, watched as his boot landed between two rattlers,
both just inches away. He was about twelve feet from Penny when
a three-foot-long snake uncoiled and struck his boot. If the animal had rattled first he might not have been so startled, but he
was and so took an awkward step and lost his balance. He put out
a hand and stopped himself from falling. A small snake found his
hand and bit. He stood up and the snake fell off. He looked at the
bite, not believing it. He looked back at Zip and reminded her to

stay. He looked at the girl, at the snakes, at his hand. Fuck, he said, fuck, fuck, fuck. He was glad the girl was deaf. He told himself to calm down. The bite pushed him on and in two steps he was on the little island with Penny.

They sat there staring straight ahead. Neither cast a glance at the other. Well, young lady, Sam said, obviously to himself. What we have here is two gallons of shit in a one-gallon bucket. He looked at his hand; there was little blood. I'll bet you're glad the big man has come to rescue you. He let out a nervous laugh, then sighed a long breath, trying to slow his panic, his heart rate. He tapped the child on the shoulder and gestured that he wanted her to get on his back. He pointed at her and then at his back. He held out his un-bitten hand and smiled. She leaned over and looked at his injured hand. He showed it to her. Yeah, he got me. I wish the fact that he was little meant something good, but it doesn't. She reached out and touched the hand, her fingers cool against his skin, small, light.

Sam turned his back slightly to her and patted his shoulder. The girl understood, put her arms around his neck, and climbed on. He stood, found her remarkably light, weightless. His hand hurt and he thought he could feel it swelling. So much for any hope that it was a dry bite. He walked less gingerly on the way back, feeling a new sense of urgency, both for the girl and for himself, also recog-nizing that his too-careful pace was the reason for his bite. He also harbored the notion that like lightning the snakes would not strike twice. That notion turned out to be wrong. After successfully kick-ing away a couple of snakes, a large one that he did not see struck and latched onto his calf just below his knee. He reached down, grabbed the snake, and hurled it away. The bite hurt like hell. Zip was barking and bouncing, but still she stayed.

Clear of the snakes, Sam gently put down the child and col-lapsed, mainly in disbelief. He was swelling at both bites and either felt or imagined some tingling in his mouth. He felt weak. He was dizzy. He stood and guided the girl back through the maze of boul-ders to his horse. He tried the radio. Static. Dusk was on now and everything was indistinct. An owl hooted somewhere. The air was much colder. Or was it chills?

By his reckoning he was six or seven miles from where he had left the sheriff. A voice scratched through the radio. He pressed the talk button. Say again. This is Innis. Nothing. In case you can hear me, I have little Penny with me. I repeat, the child is safe, unharmed and with me. However, I have managed to get myself bitten twice by rattlers. I'm about six miles southeast of the staging area. Be advised, need help. Do you read? Static. Maybe they heard me, he said to the girl. He pointed to his ear.

He opened his knapsack, which he'd tied to the saddle, and pulled out his first-aid kit. Never leave home without a snakebite kit, kid. In fact, he'd never used a kit or treated a human for a bite. Bites to horses were rare and horses were so big that they usually just got sick and got better. Considering how long it had taken him to get to the kit, it seemed a lot like closing the barn door after whatever was already out.

If only he'd been bitten only once, he'd probably be okay because of his size. But two bites, that was a different matter. He addressed the bite on his leg since it was more recent and because the snake had been bigger. He cut his pant leg with his pocket knife and ripped it up to his knee. He then swabbed the area of the bite with an antiseptic pad. He fumbled with the sterile blade, nearly dropped it when he pulled it from the plastic sleeve. He sliced through the two fang holes and used the extractor to draw out what poison he could. He hurt while he did it. For some reason, swearing helped and so he did, pleased at least that the child could not hear him. He wondered if she could swear in sign language. He finished, looked at his hand. He had reservations about using the same blade again. He decided not to. Penny watched. He stopped and listened. The world seemed quieter with her there.

Sam studied the darkening landscape. He wished he had a flare gun, then laughed at himself. He could also wish that he could teleport them back in time. If we had some ham we could have ham and eggs if we had some eggs, he said. He tried the radio again. Dale's voice scratched through.

Dale, he said.

Sam? Night air seems to help the signal.

Dale, I found her. I have her here with me.

He found her, Dale said to the others. There was cheering in the background.

She's okay, unhurt. I'm about six or so miles east and a little south of you. I wish I could be more precise.

Copy that.

Dale, I've been bitten twice by rattlers.

Jesus, Sam. How bad?

I don't know. We're going to start back. I have a flashlight burning. I'll be sticking to flat ground. Come out and try to meet us.

Roger that. We'll find you.

Leaving now.

We'll find you, Dale repeated.

Sam took off his jacket and put it around Penny. He mounted and then pulled her up into the saddle in front of him. He cantered for a while, but the horse felt uneven. The girl didn't add enough weight to be a problem. He stopped, got down, and looked at the horse's feet. The animal had a quarter crack on his left forefoot. He was hurting. If the animal came up lame, they'd be in a real fix, he thought. He left Penny in the saddle and led the horse, walking as briskly as he could. His mouth was surely tingling now. The swelling at both sites was now undeniable. He was sweating and his mouth was wet with saliva. The sweating made him cold and then there were the chills. He did not yet feel nauseated, but he knew that was coming. He wished the girl could hear and speak, because he needed the distraction of conversation to keep himself together. Zip stayed extra-close, sensing trouble. I'll be all right, girl, he said to the dog. You just keep me awake.

It was dark now. The nausea was beginning. The dizziness was more profound. He was glad he wasn't in the saddle. He'd probably

slide right off. He was worried about a lot of things now. Walking
in a straight line is hard to do, he remembered, and without a distant point of reference it is impossible. Given his disorientation there
would be no reckoning by the stars, even if he could do it. The last
thing he needed was to lead them off into the wilderness away from
where they were expected to be. He stopped the horse and brought the
girl down. He pushed down in the air with his palms, trying to say
that they would wait there. He pulled some sagebrush together into
a pile and in short order she was helping. He broke off some creosote
branches and started a fire. There was a lot of smoke at first. It stung
his eyes. He then imagined that the burning sage might cleanse him.
He fanned it over his body as he'd seen Old Dave do on many occa-
sions. He laughed at himself. He looked to find the child doing the
same thing. He pushed at the fire and watched it catch better.

He put on more branches. The fire was large now, he thought, easy
to spot from the sky or a distance. It warmed them, but it did nothing
to stop his chills. He heard a plane someplace. Penny took his hand,
his bitten hand. He looked at her, felt himself drifting. He watched
the flames, advancing, retreating, dancing, hypnotic the way flames
always are. There was Dave Wednesday, younger than he had ever
been while Sam knew him, sitting in front of a fireplace in a cabin.

You're thinking you're having a vision, aren't you? Dave said.

Pretty much. As offensive as that must be to you.

Snakebit?

Afraid so.

Dave offered Sam a mug of coffee. It's real strong, will keep you
awake for days and days. You're not a spiritual person.

That's an understatement.

Yet here you are, hallucinating stereotypes.

Pretty much. Sam drank some coffee. It was actually rather weak,
though it was too hot even to sip. So, how do I handle these bites?

You're the doctor.

I forgot. The earthquake sort of scared me. You were dead, so you
didn't feel it. It was the surprise more than anything.

I felt it. Where are the bites? Dave asked.

Back of my leg and on this hand. Little snake bit me here. He held up his hand. This is the one I'm worried about. I didn't cut into it.

Okay.

Dave held his hand and looked closely at it.

When Sam opened his eyes, he was sitting in front of the sage fire with Penny. The fire had not died down at all. He pushed some more fuel onto it. He felt the warmth of it and realized that his chills were gone. He looked at his hand. The bite marks were there, but the swelling was not. He wiggled his fingers. He looked at the girl. She was staring at the fire. He considered that he might be dreaming still. He looked through the smoke at the sky. It was a clear night, deep, black. He spotted a shooting star. He glanced to see if the child had seen it also and she had.

She made a sign that Sam assumed meant *star* or *shooting star*. He repeated it back to her.

She nodded, smiled.

Sam felt good. He pulled away the flap of his ripped trouser leg and tried to observe that bite, but couldn't see it. He put his fingers to the site of the bite and it did not feel swollen. It was not tender to his touch.

He stood and offered his hand to help Penny to her feet. Let's move, he said, and pointed west. He kicked out the fire and stood in the middle of the smoke for a few seconds. He walked over and put the girl on the horse and they walked on. After about a quarter mile, the headlights of a vehicle appeared. Sam took the flashlight he had strapped to the saddle horn and waved it back and forth.

The 4x4 stopped and three men got out. Sam couldn't make them out, but he recognized the sheriff's voice calling out to him.

When their faces were clear, Penny went running to one of the men. Sam knew it was her father. The third man was a county paramedic. Sam had seen him before, but didn't know his name.

How you doing? Dale asked.

Sam knew he looked confused, out of it, but strangely that was only because he felt perfectly fine. I think I'm okay, he said.

Let me see the bites, the paramedic said.

Sam held out his hand. The symptoms went away, he said. Just like that. No chills, no swelling, nothing.

The medic shone his light on the wound. Well, there is a bite here, all right. But there's no swelling. I don't have to tell you that's a good thing. Must have been a dry bite.

Sam nodded. He didn't mention that it had been swollen. And on the back of my leg, here. He pulled away the pant leg.

The paramedic whistled. Yep, another one. I see you cut yourself. No swelling here either. Two dry bites. I'd play the lottery tonight, if I were you. You up-to-date with your tetanus shot?

Sam said he was.

The medic had Sam sit on the ground and took his blood pressure. He whistled again. One twenty over eighty.

Dale looked at Sam's face. You all right?

Sam nodded. Apparently. He stood.

The girl's father came and hugged Sam. Thank you, he said. Thank you for finding my Penny.

You're welcome, Sam said, unsure. The fact that he felt perfectly well was unsettling and disorienting. He looked down at Penny and signed *friend*.

She signed back, but Sam didn't understand.

What did she say? Sam asked her father.

She said you will be fine now.

Sam looked at her eyes. She hugged his legs and he put his hand against her back. He dropped to a knee and hugged her back. He was so confused. He didn't know why he was not light-headed and nauseated and sweaty. Feeling healthy had never felt so strange. He looked at the father.

She's special, the man said.

Yes, she is, Sam said.

The sheriff put his hand on Sam's shoulder.

Sam looked at the stars.

I know you're exhausted.

Sam nodded but said nothing. On the contrary, he felt remarkably rested. Except for his profound confusion he felt very well. You call Sophie?

She's on her way.

The paramedic shook his head again. I ain't never seen two dry bites. The wounds don't look a bit angry.

Let's not look a gift horse in the mouth, the sheriff said. I reckon I'll ride the horse on back.

No, Dale, he's got a cracked hoof. I'll walk him back. You go back with the girl. The man moved to protest. Really, Sam said. I need to be alone with my thoughts for a short while.

Okay, Doc, you got it.

I'll stay with you, the paramedic said.

Thanks, but I want you to ride back with them.

The young man looked at the sheriff and the sheriff nodded for him to get into the vehicle.

Penny left her father and stood again in front of Sam. She signed *friend*. The one word, as if she were speaking to a child. Then she signed what Sam understood to be *thank you*.

Thank you, he said. He signed her name.

Stonefly

Years ago there had been a rope hanging from a big branch over the river and for a decade kids would swing out over the water, let go, and listen to the cheers and shouts of friends while they crashed into the pool. Then a boy named Bobby Dench tried a backflip and broke his neck. He didn't die. His family moved away, some said to Rifle, some said to Gunnison, but it was Colorado. The rope and the branch disappeared. That didn't stop sixteen-year-old Rachel Lowry from getting drunk and drowning in that very pool on the first day of autumn, 1980. She was found by her father and taken home to her mother. Her brother, Daniel, was eight at the time and watched his father appear at the edge of the yard with the rag doll that was his sister. He stood where he was, planted by the tomato garden, and watched his father fall exhausted and stricken to his knees, watched his mother scream over the girl's body, watched the family's golden retriever tug at her soaked pant leg. Daniel would not smile for six years. And when he finally did, no one knew why. It was likely he didn't either.

Daniel would saddle up every Saturday morning at six and ride down along the creek to the beaver dam. He'd cast blue wing olive patterns and catch trout after trout. He would let the fish go and catch another or perhaps the same fish, as he always let them go. His father had always insisted on it. It was preserving the home water. He would do this until noon, without any apparent joy, then ride home with his last catch of the day. He would clean it, fry it, eat it, and then go about his chores. He was a small fourteen, but he would manage without complaint the hundred-pound bales of hay and all the other work his father assigned him.

Every Saturday afternoon his mother drove him to town and waited while he sat with his therapist. Daniel didn't mind his visits to the woman. He didn't take her all that seriously. She and her husband had bought an expensive spread to live the good life and found themselves isolated and bored and now she was seeing patients a few days a week. Daniel had been with her for eighteen months, so she knew well enough what this time of year meant to him.

"Weather's nice, isn't it?" Dr. Feller said. "I love the late-summer flowers." She sipped her coffee. "So, what's been on your mind?"

"Not much. School."

"Any thoughts about your sister?" She cleared her throat. "Might as well get right to it, right?"

"I guess."

"You guess you've been thinking about her or you guess we should get right to it?"

"You're the one who put the question badly."

She scribbled on her pad. "Thoughts about your sister?"

"A few," Daniel said.

"Like what?"

"Like she's dead."

"And how do you feel about that?"

He'd been over it all before. "What do you want me to say? I don't hate her for dying. I don't resent her. I'm not even sure I miss her anymore."

The analyst scribbled.

"Want to hear about my dreams?"

"Yes, I would."

"I don't have dreams."

"Everybody dreams," she said.

"What do you dream about?" Daniel asked.

She scribbled.

"Who are those notes for?" he asked.

"For me."

"They can't be very interesting."

"Why do you say that?"

"What do you find interesting about them?"

"Why don't you tell me what you did this morning?"

"Look at last week's notes," Daniel said. "They will say that I saddled a roan gelding named Puker and went fishing. Just like every Saturday."

"Are you angry with me? About coming here?"

Daniel smiled at her. "Not at all."

"Then why the hostility?"

He looked out the window and said, calmly, "Why do you consider this hostility?"

"You don't seem pleased."

"Is a person supposed to seem pleased all the time?"

"Of course not."

"Are you pleased right now?" Daniel asked.

The therapist scribbled.

Daniel walked outside and got into the car with his mother.

"How was that?" she asked, just as she asked every Saturday. She started the Subaru.

"Fine."

"What did you talk about?"

"We talked about fishing and like that. Why do you keep bringing me here? I know you're worried that I'm talking about you in there."

"That's not true."

"Well, I'm not."

At home Daniel cleaned out the tack room like his father requested. He finished sweeping and backed into his father, who had been watching from the doorway. His father looked at the room and nodded.

"You cleaned all the saddles, too?" his father asked.

"Yes sir."

"That's too bad. Now you've got to do it twice after covering them with dust from your sweeping."

Daniel looked at the dust floating in the air, lit by the sun through the window. He didn't say anything, just put the broom aside.

His father also said nothing more, just turned and walked away and out of the barn. Daniel stood, stared at the settling dust, and set to work again on the saddles. He didn't polish the leather, merely wiped them down, but his father's point had been made. Daniel didn't think ahead. He, as always, had the order of things all turned around. He was a fuckup. He tarried in the tack room until he was certain he was late for supper.

He wandered inside to find his plate waiting for him on the kitchen table. His mother was washing the dishes. His father was lighting a fire in the fireplace shared by the kitchen and living room.

"Finished out there?" the man asked.

"All done." Daniel sat at the table.

"I can heat that up for you, if you want," his mother said.

"It's fine, thanks."

When the fire was burning his parents went into the living room and sat in front of it. Daniel studied their legs through the window of orange light while he chewed on cold chicken. They sat close together, but did not touch.

The next morning, after feeding the horses and cleaning out the water barrels, Daniel saddled Puker and rode to the beaver dam to find that in the night it had broken in several places. He imagined a bear or maybe a wolf—they were around again—but he really had no clue. It changed the stream's face. He rode back against the current, studying the mud and the foam. He stopped finally and fished a riffle, using a zug bug, which he had always thought of as cheating. He stood midstream and covered the fast water without success. However, the creek's newness was startling and he found himself leaving Puker to munch grass while he hiked upstream. He spent the

better part of the morning being seduced by lie after lie until he remembered the horse. He put his line back on his reel and realized
he was not so far now from the pool where his sister had drowned.
He had not been back there since her death. He thought he could see
the big cottonwood that once held the swinging rope. He thought
about his therapist and how this was just the sort of thing she'd want
to hear about and he knew he'd never tell her. He'd never tell her, because it didn't amount to anything. He didn't feel a thing and had
no thought beyond recognition of that place. He turned around and
fished his way downstream and to his horse. The horse was standing
when he found his way back but was nervous.

"Whoa, boy," he said to the gelding. He picked up the reins, feeling that at any second the animal might bolt. Daniel looked around,
wondered if the bear that had possibly wrecked the beaver dam was
still around. He was glad he didn't have a rifle with him. If there was a
bear and he was armed he might do something stupid like shoot it. His
father always said that shooting a bear would only make it angry. He
mounted the nervous horse and steadied him, rode away slowly. The
last thing he wanted to do was drive quickly toward the beast if he happened to be nosing around. He never saw a bear or any sign.

The week passed, as weeks pass, but he did not ride out to fish. His
parents thought this odd, were alarmed into silence by it, and his
therapist asked him if he was angry, saying at the end, "You know,
it's okay to be angry." Daniel walked through his days not quite as
nervous as a green horse. Finally on a Saturday in mid-October he
was saddled and riding to the creek, not to his usual spot, but to the
place above, nearer his house, where his sister had drowned. He saw
that the last riffle he'd fished was submerged now. The beavers must
have repaired their dam and lodge. He had little desire to put his rod
together. He sat in his saddle and stared at the water, at the brush on
the other side and finally upstream at the big cottonwood. He studied the tree for a couple of minutes, long enough for the time to seem
long, and nudged his horse to take a step in that direction.

He dismounted and stepped to the edge of the widest stretch of the stream. The beach there, what little of it was still exposed, was mud and pebbles. The willows on the far side were half-submerged. The water over there moved steadily, but the pool appeared calm, un-stirred. A flash caught his eye, a big flash, unmistakably the showing of the underside of a fish, but so large. He thought the sudden-ness of it might have made him see it as larger, but then it flashed again. The trout was not rising to take food, but it cruised by again. Daniel sat beneath the cottonwood and watched the pool, counted four more appearances of the fish, easily the largest trout he had ever seen in the creek. Still, however, he made no move for his fly rod. He watched until the fish showed no more. He mounted and rode on home.

That night at dinner, Daniel asked his father, "What's the biggest trout you've ever seen in the creek?"

"Years ago I hooked one that was thirteen, maybe fourteen inches, but I didn't land him. He took off downstream through a riffle."

"I think I saw one that's at least twenty inches. I think bigger."

"I think your eyes are playing tricks on you. That creek can't sup-port a fish that big."

"I'm pretty sure."

"Catch it and bring it to me and I'll believe you."

Daniel didn't like being doubted, but he had to admit that he doubted himself. He looked at his father and didn't feel anger, but he felt profound disappointment. "I think I will catch it," he said.

His father laughed. "You do that."

Daniel ceased paying attention in his classes, enough so that his par-ents were informed. They could not hide their terror. Daniel under-stood it. They had lost one child. Daniel realized as his mother and father at once pounced upon him and stayed clear of him that he had never known the circumstances of his sister's death. And so, one night at dinner, he terrified them further.

"Just how did Rachel die?" Daniel asked.

"She drowned," his mother said.

"How did she drown?"

"I'm afraid she had been drinking."

"Why was she out there? Why had she been drinking?"

Daniel's father cleared his throat. "It seems your sister had a problem with alcohol. She was an alcoholic. We didn't know. We didn't see it. We should have seen it."

Daniel stabbed at the meat on his plate a few times. "Are you an alcoholic?" Daniel asked his father.

The man breathed deeply.

Daniel's mother put her hand on his father's arm.

"You drink. Are you an alcoholic?"

"I do drink, son, but I'm not an alcoholic."

Daniel nodded.

"I drank more after your sister died," the man said.

Daniel looked through the window at the dusk turning to night. "I remember that Rachel would scream a lot."

"Rachel had some problems," Daniel's mother said.

"Are you saying she killed herself?"

"No, of course not," she said. "It was an accident."

Daniel looked at them, one then the other. He looked down at his hardly touched food. "I'm going to camp out tonight."

"What?"

"It's freezing out there."

"I'll be all right. I need to think."

"Where are you going to camp?" his father asked.

"Not far. I just want to be outside. I just want to listen to the creek while I sleep."

"I don't think it's a good idea."

"I want to do it."

His parents looked at each other.

"If you need to, do it," his father said. "But we need to know where you'll be."

"By the big cottonwood."

Daniel watched his parents exchange terrified glances. His father lifted his water glass and then set it down without drinking.

"Why there?" the man asked.

"I'll be there tonight."

"I don't understand," his mother said. "It's too cold to camp out."

"I'll be fine."

"I won't allow it," his father said.

Daniel just stared at the man. He wasn't angry. He wasn't frustrated or excited. But neither was he calm. "That's where I'll be."

"Maybe I should call your doctor," his mother said. "You should talk to her first, before you do anything."

"She's an idiot."

"Can we just talk about this?" his mother asked.

"No."

Daniel's father looked out the window at the darkness and said nothing. He slowly squared himself to the table again and began eating.

Puker was unhappy at being taken away from his feed and saddled in the dark. The gelding complained but relaxed under the currycomb. Daniel didn't have much gear, just a one-person tent, his sleeping bag, and his fishing gear. He took his father's fly-tying kit with him as well.

He built a fire at streamside to warm up. That gave him enough light to set up his tent. He stared at the yellow-and-green structure in the firelight. Daniel had considered sleeping out in his bag without it, but he'd never been comfortable like that. Somehow the cocoon of a tent made him feel safe, even though he knew it afforded protection from only wind, rain, and snow. He recalled a joke he'd heard: What does a bear call a man in a tent? A burrito. Whether it was true or not he imagined that the bears were up high and hibernating. Burrito or no, he crawled into his tortilla and tried to sleep. As long as his horse wasn't screaming, he figured all was well. He managed to get warm in his bag and did drift off.

The rustling was faint at first. Then near. He thought he heard sniffing at the base of his tent. He imagined a coyote, maybe a wolf. He took a peek out into the dawn and mist and saw a cow moose drinking from the creek. He relaxed a bit and then realized that there was a bull with her, standing knee deep in the water. He didn't like bull moose. No one did. Bull moose were dangerous. They were not the Bullwinkles that city people imagined. Daniel wanted to wait them out, but he needed to relieve himself. He found a twig at the mouth of his tent and snapped it. The bull raised his head. Daniel froze. The bull seemed to look straight at him. He didn't know what he might do if the animal charged.

The stillness was disturbed by a loud splash. Then another. Bull and cow ran away, upstream and then across through the willows. Daniel pulled himself out and stared at the water, saw the flash of a big trout's belly. He fell and began to feel the frigid air. He hopped around slapping his arms while he got the fire going. He ate his bologna sandwich and studied the creek.

He watched the big fish make rise after rise for no apparent food. It was still so cold that no insects were available. Daniel imagined or perhaps hoped that there would be a few mayflies later, after the sun had warmed things up a bit. But there would certainly be gnats. There were always gnats.

Daniel considered giving Puker a good brushing, as he hadn't done it when arriving in the night, but he did not. He gave him some grain that he'd brought and tied him out to graze.

Daniel fed the fire, made it big and hot and enjoyed the brisk cold on his back while he toasted his arms and face. An eagle flew by far overhead. After that a few chatty ravens flew past as if to steal a good look at him. He was apparently not all that interesting. He didn't need ravens to tell him that.

He heard Puker stir, then whinny. He'd been sitting for a couple of hours, warm now, lost in something like thought. He listened and could hear the creaking of a truck bouncing across the rough part of the track just after the fjord. He got up to settle the horse while the vehicle arrived. As he expected, it was his parents, but wedged in between them on the bench of the pickup was his therapist, Dr. Feller.

The three sat, framed behind the windshield, seemingly frozen, as he must have seemed to them. They looked alarmingly alike behind the glass. Daniel released the horse's halter and the animal returned to grazing. The trio spilled out of the truck and approached him in wandering paths, his mother taking the most direct one. His father wandered away from the stream, pretending, at least, to survey the hills and the clouds gathering far off. His doctor, as she liked to be known, veered toward the stream, staring at it as if she'd never seen one before. She was the first to speak.

"I see you're camping out."

Daniel nodded. He looked at his mother. "I'll be home directly."

"I don't like you being out here like this," his father said.

"I'm just thinking," Daniel said.

"What are you thinking about?" his therapist asked.

"Things." Daniel was curt, perhaps dismissive, but he didn't think he was being rude. Not that he cared. "Stuff fourteen-year-old boys think about."

"Oh," Dr. Feller said.

"I haven't masturbated yet," he said. That was rude.

He looked at his mother. She appeared to have been slapped. "Well, I haven't."

His father cleared his throat. "I've had about enough of this."

"I'll be home soon," Daniel said again.

His therapist walked closer to him but kept stealing glances back at the pool. "You know, it's all right to be angry."

"So I've been told. I'll give that some thought. Three o'clock. I'll get angry at three. Will that work for you?"

"Daniel," his mother said. "Dr. Feller is just trying to help."

"I don't need any help," he said. "I'm only fourteen, but I can see that this therapy crap is for you two. I was eight. The only feeling I ever had about any of this is confusion. I don't want to know anything.

I don't want to figure out anything. I just want you to know that I'm not out here to drown myself."

"We know that, son." The relief on his father's face was clear. Still, he was angry, perhaps at being defied, perhaps at being made to feel afraid.

"This is good, Daniel, this is good," Dr. Feller said.

"Shut up," Daniel said.

"Daniel," his mother said.

"Tell her to get in the truck," Daniel said to his parents. "I'm sick of being one of the doctor's hobbies."

He could not have hit the woman any harder with a steel pipe or a brick. She turned and walked, red-faced, to the truck.

"I really need to be alone right now. I'll probably be here most of the day. I might stay another night."

"You warm enough?" his father asked.

"I'm fine." His mother started to ask something, but he stopped her. "Really, I'm fine."

No one said anything else. The three drove away and Daniel watched them until they were out of sight. He then turned to regard the same clouds his father had been watching. Snow was coming.

The mayfly hatch that Daniel had imagined, or hoped for, still had not materialized at noon. A few small trout were rising to midges at the outer edge of the pool. Occasionally the big fish would surface, roll, and disappear. He got himself into his neoprene waders and boots. He took a size twenty midge from his box and snipped off the hook. He didn't want to land the fish, only have it take his lure. But the fish did not. After several casts small fish came up to investigate; a few even mouthed the fly and spat it out.

The day did not warm up much, but acted in a way consistent with his prediction of snow. He tried other flies, choices that made no sense. He tried wildly colored salmon flies and received no interest at all. The same was true of streamers that he swung along the outer edge of the pool with the current and beaded nymphs that dropped down deep into the stillest section of the water. The big trout continued to show itself time and again, two or three times with a splash.

At around four o'clock a bit of snow began to fall. Daniel collected wood and got his fire going again. He put some big logs on. He opened his fly box and took out a size eight stonefly, a fly he never would have used in this creek or at this time of year.

Again he used his wire cutters to snap off the end of the hook. He tied the fly onto the tippet and roll cast the fly upstream and to the far side of the pool. Even with his best technique, the fact that his rod was so light made the big lure splash like a stone into the water and sent mad ripples all through the pool. He thought he'd have to pull his line in and rest the water for at least a half hour. But then he saw the big shape coming, circling around, then venturing close to the stonefly imitation. The trout seemed to regard it but swam past. He reeled in and threw the line back out, splashing again, and again the trout came and gave another disdainful glance. This went on until it became clear that the animal would not bite. All he wanted was for the fish to put his mouth to the fly.

He returned to the fire and added more fuel. He took out the tying kit and started making a larger stonefly. He tied it onto a number six hook. He made the abdomen fat, laying the mustard-colored dubbing on thick, then stopped to stare at the thread dangling there from the vise, the bobbin swinging. He took the little scissors and snipped some of his own black hair. He applied more wax to the thread and worked his curling hairs onto it, mixing it with the dubbing. He finished the fly without bothering to fashion any legs for the thing. He wound the grizzly hackle onto the fly and tied it off. He cemented the head and sat back. The snow was falling harder. He looked up at it and wanted to find it beautiful.

This time he did not remove the hook. In fact, he didn't even crimp down the barb as he always did. As long as he had been fishing, he had never eaten a trout from this stream. He cast the fly out and it disturbed the water awfully. But as soon as it landed, the big fish was on it. The trout bit the fly and pulled it deep. Daniel suffered from trigger lock. He was frozen, shocked. He finally gave a yank to set the hook. The trout took off downstream. Daniel stepped into the water to follow it, getting the line on his reel as quickly as possible. The line went slack and he was sure he'd lost the trout, but the fish had simply come back, pulled the line taut as it fought upstream. This back-and-forth happened three more times, all the while Daniel fearing that he was going to wear the fish out and be unable to safely release it. He tried to ease up on the pressure and let the animal slip the hook, but it wouldn't happen. However, what he feared did happen. The exhausted trout stopped racing, stopped pulling, and let itself be reeled in.

Daniel stepped to the bank. It was the darker side of dusk now, and the snow was really coming down. It was much colder and Daniel could feel it profoundly because he was wet from perspiration. He held the trout in the shallow water. It was huge. It was easily over two feet long. Its presence just didn't make any sense. None of it made sense. He'd caught the fish on his little four-weight rod and 7x tippet. It didn't make sense that the trout would take this fly, especially when the lure had been presented so badly, especially when the fish had refused the same thing previously. The fish huffed. The rainbow coloring was beautiful, but the thing was somewhat hideous for its size.

He pulled it fully onto the beach and worked the hook out of its mouth. It seemed to look at him. And he of course looked back. He cut the fly from his line and put all the line on the reel. He broke down his rod.

He walked back up the slope to his camp, pulled off his waders, and laced on his boots. He quietly put out his fire. With the snow falling he was happy to extinguish only the flames. He struck his tent, packed his gear. He saddled his horse and was ready to leave.

He walked back to the edge of the pool and looked down at the fish. Remarkably, it was still alive, but he left it where it was, where it needed to be. After all, he thought, it couldn't have been there in the first place.

As Daniel rode home, he leaned his head back and looked at the sky. For all he knew the snowflakes were stars, and he smiled.

A High Lake

Norma Snow still rode. She chose a shorter mount, almost a pony, and used a synthetic saddle; a leather roper was just too much to lift, but she still rode. Her horse was a fourteen-hand Arabian, twelve years old, a little loose in the back, with sturdy feet. She called the gelding Zed because of his lightning-bolt-shaped blaze. Norma lived alone in the house that she had built and shared with her husband. He was dead now. She hired a nurse to come by once every day to make sure she was still upright and not stretched out helpless on the kitchen floor. Norma wanted the nurse for no more than that.

Norma rode every morning. Her doctor told her that riding was perhaps not a good idea because of her brittle bones, her osteoporosis. She ignored him. Hell, at her age walking around wasn't a good idea, she'd told him. Yes, she took the Fosamax, but she still saddled up every morning at six, rain, snow, or sunshine, dark or light, foggy or clear, and rode out through the land she now leased to neighboring ranchers. She kept no cattle of her own. She rode out through the dumb cows, across the expanse of meadow, up the hill, along the ridge, and then up to the high lake, a pond, really. If she ever took too long and the nurse arrived before her return, the poor man would have no idea what to do. That was how Norma wanted it. Dying in the saddle was a romantic way to go, she thought.

She made her way along the last steep stretch of trail to the lake. She had once, years ago, seen a cow moose up there with a yearling calf. She now approached every morning with the hope that she might see another pair. The stiff, cold breeze blew in from the northwest.

Zed, knowing the drill, turned to put his left flank toward the hillside, where Norma easily dismounted. She fastened the top button on her field coat. The coming cold weather didn't trouble her; it was not even unwelcome; it simply was a fact. Your horse steps in a puddle, his hoof gets wet. It's not a good thing, it's not a bad thing, it's just a thing. She remembered her husband saying that from time to time. She watched Zed as she stepped away. He stood on a dropped rein better than most horses stood hitched to a post.

She approached the acre of water and observed the wind riffling the surface. She sat on her favorite flat rock, imagined that years of her visits had molded the stone to fit her wide bottom. The breeze was bothering the water, but not enough to hide the trout swimming near her. The trout up here, where there was so little pressure, were cagey, but they were accustomed to this figure perched by the bank every morning. Her husband had loved and cursed the difficult-to-catch fish. His voice used to come back to her more often, sharing his thoughts about horses and fishing. But now he did not speak that much. For nearly eight years she had been alone with her horse and her thoughts. She liked that they were her thoughts. They came like a glacier, moving slowly, and like any glacier they were a tsunami of ice, surging, unstoppable. She had completed a catalog of the bird life on her place, with notes of songs and seasonal habits. She had finally read Proust and decided she did not like him, had decided the same about Henry James, had decided that Eudora Welty would have been her friend, and had come to think that Hemingway was not all that bad. Recently she had painted an acrylic on canvas of the hind end of an elk. When her nurse, Braden, saw it, he said, "Why'd you paint a deer's ass?"

Norma sipped her tea and leaned back in her chair. "First of all, it's an elk. I painted his butt because that all I ever see of him."

She hadn't hired Braden because he was smart but because he was just what he was, a big wall of meat with a box of blond hair for a head, strong enough to lift her off the floor if need be and capable of stabbing 9-1-1 with one of those kielbasas he called fingers. Braden

lived in a double-wide trailer on the southern edge of Laramie and
not too far away from Norma's place, so weather was never much of
an issue for him getting there.

Norma watched the trout rise to take an ant that had fallen from
a blade of grass. Her eyes came back to the bank and followed it to a
place where animals would come to drink. The muddy ground there
was a little more chewed up than usual. She walked over to look at
the tracks. She found the cloven hoofprints of deer and elk and another set, a set of horse tracks. The tracks were clearly from a horse
and an unshod horse at that. She kneeled down and traced the indentation with a finger. The tracks were the freshest of the sets, having fallen on top of the others. All the trails up here were steep and
rocky, so even the horses with the sturdiest feet wore at least hind
shoes. She hadn't heard of anyone turning out horses in years. Even
her husband had stopped. It seemed a little early to do it anyway.
She tried to follow the tracks, lost them on the carpet of grass, then
found them again on a deer path. She couldn't read much into the
tracks, but she imagined a horse about the size of her Zed.

She climbed back into the saddle and followed the trail. She followed the sign off the worn path and south down toward a narrow
arroyo that she rarely visited. The tracks were easy to see, clear and
clean. She even noted that the animal dragged its left forefoot slightly
and that it had a sizable chunk missing from the outside wall of the
hind foot on the same side. As she reached the bottom of the drainage she realized that she had seen no droppings. She'd followed the
sign for at least four miles and had not seen one apple of horseshit.

She looked at her watch. It was nine thirty. Braden would be at
her house about now, pacing and worried more about what to do than
about her. She headed back in a slow canter that felt good. She slowed
Zed to a walk at the edge of the clearing and then dismounted, loos-
ening the girth, to lead him the last hundred yards.

She came up to the stable across the yard from her back door.
Braden was in fact there. He came out of the kitchen waving his
arms like a fool.

"I was worried," he said in an admonishing tone.

"Thought you might be. That's why I didn't rush back."

"What happened?"

"I was riding."

"You okay?"

Norma nodded.

"Next time could you leave a note?"

Norma released the cinch and put the stirrup up over the horn. "Let's try this: you learn not to worry?"

"Yes ma'am."

"You can see I'm still standing, so you might as well go on home."

She watched as he walked back to his Nissan Sentra with the unpainted quarter panel. His big blond head hung.

"Braden," she called.

He stopped and turned to face her.

"Thanks for worrying."

"Yes ma'am."

A couple of hours later, Norma sat down at her table to have lunch. Egg salad. Pat Hilton, from a neighboring ranch, knocked as she entered through the kitchen's Dutch door. The large woman did that a couple of times a week and Norma didn't much mind. She was a plump fifty-year-old with blond hair that resisted graying. As an attempt at humor, the woman would point out not infrequently that her husband was not a hotel Hilton.

"Hey, lady," Pat said.

"Sit down and have some egg salad with me." Norma nodded to the chair across from her.

"Don't mind if I do. Don't mind if I do." The woman made herself a plate and sat. "So, where's Braden?"

"Sent him home."

"You pay that man to come up here every day, for what? Forty minutes? Twenty minutes?"

"Less than that, if possible. Hell, if he sees me standing in the yard and waves, he can keep on going as far as I'm concerned."

"That's crazy."

"He does what I pay him to do. He's only knitting with one needle, but he does what I ask him to do."

"I still say it's crazy."

"It would be crazy having to make conversation with him for hours, having him traipse around here trying to help and getting in the way."

"I could use some help."

"I take help when I need it," Norma said. Norma took a bite, looked out the window. "You folks missing a horse? Turn any out early?"

Pat shook her head, her big mouth full. "We had a mare colic last week. She almost died. Dan had to get up all through the night to make sure she didn't lay down and get all twisted up."

Lie down, Norma corrected the woman in her head.

"I see your step is fixed. Braden do that?"

"I can measure and cut a board and drive nails as well as anybody." Norma took a deep breath and again peered out the window at the ridge far off. "So, how's your daughter?"

"She hates me. At least, this week. Because I won't drive her down to Denver and I won't let her go with her friends. Fort Collins isn't good enough. Has to be Denver."

"What's in Denver?"

"Shopping. Movies, I guess. The fact that it's not here."

Norma nodded. "It's tough being a ranch kid."

"Being a ranch mom ain't no picnic either."

Norma gave up a solidarity nod that wasn't completely sincere. Norma had loved the ranch and the ranch life. She'd loved it when her husband had been alive and after. They'd lost their twelve-year-old daughter to leukemia. And she still loved the place. They almost lost the ranch when they lost most of their cattle to a blizzard. That was after their daughter's death and they refused to give up. They couldn't leave it. Both her daughter and her husband were buried on the ranch. She would be as well, but she had no idea who would be there to watch the weeds grow over their graves. She had no family left to whom to leave the land.

"You would think she'd be happy to go to Fort Collins," Pat said about her daughter.

"She'll be off to college soon," Norma offered as a salve.

"It won't be too soon, I can tell you that," Pat said. She shook her head, perhaps recognizing her own lie. "Listen to me railing on so." She stopped talking and ate her lunch.

Norma thought about the tracks out there. She had a notion to saddle up and ride Zed back out and search for more sign. But she wouldn't do that. Her bones didn't want her to do it. Besides, the farrier was coming that afternoon.

She said good-bye to Pat and cleaned the dishes. She then went into the den and sat in her good chair, put up her feet, and let her body rest. She thumbed through a regional bird guide and drifted into a nap.

Norma awoke to the sound of tires on the gravel of her drive. She pushed herself to standing and heard herself groan. It was a complaint she was certain she issued frequently, but this time she heard it. The driver outside tapped a beep on the horn. Norma grabbed her glasses and stepped outside.

The little round farrier was out of his truck and waddling toward the barn. He turned at the sound of the door.

"Afternoon, Norma."

"Bob."

Bob was still wearing the black rodeo rib protector he wore when driving. "I was going to grab your beast."

"I'll get him for you."

"I'll get my tools."

Norma went into the barn and grabbed Zed's halter from the nail outside his stall. The horse was munching the last of his hay. She collected him and led him out into the yard. She stroked his muzzle and rubbed his ears while the farrier worked. He'd taken off his rib protector.

"Tell me," Norma said, "why do you wear that vest?"

"I like the weight of it," he said. "Also, if I'm ever in a crash that vest will protect me from my own damn air bag. Did you know that those things open at around two hundred miles per hour? The blink of an eye. And I'm short. Maybe you've noticed that I'm a short man. I'm sitting pretty damn close to that steering wheel. The blink of an eye."

Norma nodded.

Bob liked to talk and she'd opened the door. That was okay with Norma. It meant she didn't have to make conversation. He'd follow one scent for a while and then pick up another.

"Yessiree Bobby," he said. "They're going to save us to death. Of course you know that the propellant that shoots the bag open with nitrogen gas is toxic and explosive."

Norma said nothing.

"Yep. Sodium azide. Just a couple of grams ingested could kill you. Yep. It's a big problem. All them cars in the junkyards are eventually going to leak that stuff into the environment. When the bag deploys it becomes nitrogen and sodium, harmless. The problem is when they don't deploy. Yep."

And so it went. Through the taking off of the old shoes, the cutting, the clipping, the rasping, the hammering, and the nailing. He snipped off the tip of the last nail while yakking about how some folks consider tomatoes to be poisonous because they are of the nightshade family. Bob stood and arched his back in a stretch.

"All done?" Norma asked.

"We're all done." Bob looked at the sunset just starting. "What do you think? Snow soon?"

"I reckon." Norma took the horse back to his stall while Bob picked up his tools. When she came back he was slipping into his vest. She pulled some bills from her pocket and paid him.

"Exact as always," he said.

That night Norma awoke with pains in her back and hip. She took a couple of the pills that seldom seemed to abate the pain, but did usually put her to sleep. Tonight, though, she just lay there on her back, staring at the ceiling, imagining that what she was thinking was a dream. She thought of the tracks and the horse that made them. In her mind it was a young mare, an overo Paint, brown and white. She could see her drinking from the pond. She could see her raising her head at the sound of something in the brush. She was moderately stout with a big rump. She walked away from the water and disappeared into the trees.

The morning was much colder. Norma felt it in her bones even before she pushed herself out of the covers. It was mornings like this, when her bare feet hit the cold wood of the floor, that she remembered her last dog, Zach. The German shepherd had lived for fourteen years. At the end, he'd been unable to climb onto the bed and so would push himself as close to her bedside as he could. She would swing her feet down in the morning and find his warm body beneath her. She recalled pausing there and feeling the dog's chest rise and fall through the soles of her feet. She loved him and she'd let him live too long. He'd been blind, deaf, and barely able to walk, and she'd let one more day go by, then another, not able to bear the thought of putting him down. Now she cursed herself, wondering how she could have let him suffer so.

She was up a good hour earlier than usual. It was still dark. After a small breakfast, yogurt and a banana, and a brief listen to the radio weather, a mere confirmation of what she already knew, that it was cold, she packed a thermos of coffee, some bread and cheese.

She walked out to the barn and to Zed's stall. She clumsily took the blanket off him and draped it over his gate. She led him out of the barn, brushed him out, and saddled him. She put her lunch in a saddlebag and strapped it on. She mounted with some difficulty, her hip complaining, and rode out.

The birds were just beginning to chatter, but when she hit the tree line, they stopped. The stillness held for a moment, then the birds started up again. A rabbit or a squirrel disturbed some leaves. Norma rode with her eyes pressed to the sides of the trail, looking up occasionally to reassure Zed that she was paying attention. She remembered her husband telling her that somebody had to steer the horse and it should probably be the rider. Some clouds hung like webbing in the trees ahead of her, but she felt warmer than she had at home. In fact, she felt light; her bones did not speak to her. She discovered what she thought might be tracks leading off from a patch of mossy ground. The trail stopped but they gave her a direction and it was up. She forgot the ground and paid attention to guiding Zed up the mountain. Some of the going was steep and rocky and the short horse stumbled more than once, but her confidence pushed him on. When she finally came to a place where she could see out of the trees she was astonished to find that she did not recognize what was below her. She looked back at the way she had come and that path seemed clear to her, so she did not become afraid. Still, she dismounted and set up a rock marker.

Norma was miles from home, much farther than she had meant to go. She admitted to herself that she was now lost. Clouds were gathering in the west and blowing her way. Snow was coming. She could feel it, but strangely not in her bones. She didn't even feel tired or sore from the strenuous ride. She rode on, figuring that she would probably come up and over and see below her the river that ran between her place and the Hiltons'.

First she saw the animal trail, followed it, and then she found the tracks, clearly a horse's, clearly those of the same animal she'd tracked the day before. She climbed down from the saddle and traced evidence of the damage to the rear hoof with her fingers. The indentation felt warm. She felt warm. She stood and climbed easily back onto Zed. She paused and observed the fact and then quickly chose to forget it. She looked at her watch and thought about poor Braden showing up, remaining patient for an hour or so and then panicking. He would walk the pasture and then call the sheriff. They would be out and looking for her by late afternoon. But she felt no urgency about getting back.

She followed the sign. Then she heard the falls. She was surprised, but at least she now knew where she was. The hoofprints followed the stream up to the pond at the base of the falls, then became hard to read, appearing to circle and slip into the water. And so that's what Norma did.

Zed didn't want to, but Norma pressed him and he complied. They stepped through the frigid, falling water, Zed breaking into an unrequested canter to get through quickly. Norma even let out a bit of a yelp. She slapped the horse's neck and said, "That was bracing, wasn't it, boy?" She looked up and there was what looked to be a cave, but it wasn't a cave; there was light at the other side of it. It was a huge hole in the rock wall, big enough to ride through. Again Zed resisted, but she pushed on through the muddy floor and out into a different place altogether. The sky was blue, not slate gray. The air was warm and snow threatened, but no wind blew.

She rode through a meadow filled with fairy trumpets and purple lupines and newly bloomed chickweed. She could see fireweed crowding a slope in the distance. The flowers didn't make sense altogether, and the chickweed should have been long gone. The meadow was thick with wheatgrass and brome. Zed had noticed the grass as well. Norma stopped and let him drop his head to graze while she surveyed the landscape and the cloudless sky. Then she spotted movement in the brush on a slope. She thought at first it was a mountain lion and then saw it was a dog, a young dog bounding, a German shepherd. The dog came closer, barking, playing. It could have been Zach, the way he looked, the way he crouched and leaped. She dismounted, rested on a knee, and called the dog.

The animal came to her. He couldn't have been older than two years. She rubbed his ears and the feeling made her happy. He had no collar. "Whose boy are you?" she asked and looked around for the owner. "So, where the hell am I, eh, fella?" she asked the dog. She left Zed standing on his rein and walked with the dog toward a gentle slope. She felt strong, loose, and she gained the crest of the ridge without becoming winded. She looked down at a verdant and amazing valley, a valley she had never seen before, junipers and scrub on the hills, hardwood trees along and between two moderately fast-flowing rivers that became one slowly twisting body. There was a beaver dam on a creek and birds everywhere.

The dog pranced around her. Norma watched the shepherd, listened to his bark, observed the way he slightly favored his left front paw. Just like her Zach. She felt excited and frightened by this. She had watched Zach grow old and die and yet this animal was just like her young pet. She scratched his neck and turned him over and there was a scar on his belly, a scar from when he'd been cut by barbed wire when he was a young pup. Zach. This dog had the same scar. Norma felt dizzy, lost, then happy. She stood, turned, and looked down at Zed grazing.

Her mind didn't exactly race, but it made many stops. She was lost, that much she accepted. The weather was so very different here. She understood that there were often microclimates that were observably different from adjacent ones, but this was so much more. The dog was remarkably similar to her Zach, but it couldn't be him. But it was him. And if it was him, then where was she? If it was Zach, then what else was possible? She stared back at the rivers below. The jagged white of the fast water appeared to spell something, but of course it didn't. Zach was dead. Zach was dead, she kept telling herself. But this dog had Zach's scar. What else was here? She slipped out of her jacket, sat, and the dog lay down beside her.

She found herself searching the air for a familiar scent, any familiar scent. There was none. She stared. She listened. She imagined trout in the water below her. She imagined the whistling of her husband as he fished. She imagined the footfalls of her daughter coming up the hill behind her. She tried to smell her. Somehow she knew that if she smelled her child, she would be real. She put her face to the dog and sniffed. She couldn't tell if he smelled like Zach.

Time was getting away from her. The sheriff had the helicopter up now. Neighbors were no doubt on horseback searching for her. Braden was pacing the yard, useless to do anything else. Then it occurred to her that the light was not changing, the sun was where it had been when she first rode into this place. She was frightened suddenly, but then the feeling was gone and she was empty, but not really, as she expected something, someone. She was ashamed to think it, so she said her daughter's name. "Nathalie." She said her husband's name. "Howard." No scents followed the breeze to her. No whistling, no singing, no whispering, no footfalls. But the dog was here. Zach was here.

Norma looked down at Zed and at the way they had come in. The horse whinnied and stepped nervously. Norma stood and the dog lay still and remained still while she walked down the slope to the meadow. The dog raised only his head as she peered up at him from Zed's side. She checked the cinch and mounted. She sat there for a few minutes, then turned the horse and headed back.

She found the gap in the wall and rode through and came out under the falls, the water shockingly cold, to find it snowing, to find the air frigid, the sky a steel gray. From the falls she knew the general way home, though she still considered herself lost. She rode for nearly an hour, when above the trees she heard the distant chopping of a helicopter. The noise grew closer but there was no way she could be seen in the dense forest. The snow fell harder and her bones complained. What she realized was that she was disoriented, not simply because she was lost, but because she could not reasonably process where she had just found herself. In fact, the awareness of her feeling adrift made her feel more so.

She came to a clearing and someone called to her. A man's voice, hoarse with the cold air and concern, found her and she held up.

"Norma!" It was Dan Hilton.

"Hey there, Dan," she said. "I suppose I've gotten a lot of people worried. I'm a little cold."

"Where's your coat?" he asked. He had his parka quickly off and put around the old woman.

"I don't know," she said. She hadn't realized she'd forgotten it at the lake. All of a sudden her disorientation was real and profound.

Dan spoke into his two-way radio, but Norma didn't hear any of what he was saying. "Let's get you home," he said to her. "You okay to ride or you want me to lead him?"

"I'm okay. Let's go."

Norma followed the man down a familiar ravine, up over a ridge, and then she was looking down at her pastures. The snow was falling heavily. In the yard were parked a paramedic's vehicle, a sheriff's car, and Braden's Nissan. Pat Hilton and her daughter were there also.

Braden ran out to meet her. "Mrs. Snow, are you all right?" He turned to Dan. "Mr. Hilton, is she okay?"

"I think so," Dan said.

In the yard, the medic and the sheriff's deputy helped her down from the saddle. "Easy does it," the medic said.

Pat hovered close. "You're going to be fine, dear," she said. "Just fine. We'll take good care of you."

Norma looked past Pat at her daughter, standing near the medic's truck with her arms folded across her chest.

"You gave us a scare, Mrs. Snow," the deputy said.

"I'm sorry," she said, absently.

"Well, let's get you in the house," the medic said.

Inside, the medic took off his gloves and gently felt Norma's face and neck. He checked her pulse, took her temperature, and measured her blood pressure. Pat brought in a cup of tea.

"That's good," the medic said. "She's cold. Suffered a bit of exposure out there. Another blanket, too."

"I'll get one," Pat said.

"I need to ask you some questions, Mrs. Snow, okay?"

Norma nodded.

"Do you know who I am?"

Norma studied the man's face for a long second. "Yes, you're the boy who rode the goat."

"What was that?"

"You're the boy who fell off the goat," she said.

Pat was back with the blanket. "What in the world is she talking about? Is she delirious?"

The medic laughed. "No, I rode in the goat race when I was a kid and I had a pretty good wreck. Broke my clavicle."

"You didn't have a beard then," Norma said, smiled.

"No ma'am, I didn't. I was eight." He stood and began to put away his sphygmomanometer. "She's all right. Pretty cold out there, Mrs. Snow? How'd you lose your coat?"

"Can't tell you," she said. "It's out there somewhere."

"Remember why you took it off?"

Norma shook her head.

"Well, the thing now is to keep covered up and stay warm. Keep drinking hot liquids."

"I'll see to it," Pat said. "I'll get a hot water bottle for her feet."

"That's good."

Dan came into the house with some wood and went about making a fire in the stove insert. "We'll get it toasty in here," he said.

The medic put his hand on Norma's shoulder. "I'll swing by tomorrow morning and check on you."

"Thank you," Norma said.

"I'll stay with her," Pat said.

"No, you won't," Norma said.

"Norma."

"You heard me. I'm nobody's baby and I live alone and that's how I will live tonight."

"It might be advisable to have someone stay with you, ma'am," the medic said. "Just to be on the safe side."

"No."

"Ma'am? You might be a little disoriented."

"Do I seem disoriented now?"

"Braden, he can stay," Dan said.

"Hell no," Norma said. "Thank you all for everything, but I'm warming up now and I feel just fine. You're Dan. You're Pat. You're the goat boy and that wall of beef out there is Braden. It's Thursday and it's snowing and I got lost. And though that might be stupid, it's not a crime."

"All right, Norma," Dan said, putting his hand on Pat's back and starting her toward the door. "Keep the phone beside you in case you need to call. You'll do that for us?"

"Okay."

"And I'm going to call and check on you," Pat said. "So, answer." Norma nodded.

They left and Braden came into the house.

"I brushed out Zed and put him away," he said. "I made sure he got him some extra grain."

"You put his blanket on him?"

"Yes ma'am."

"The blue one?"

"Yes ma'am."

"Thank you, Braden. Thanks a lot. You can go on home now. Sorry I took up your day."

"I told my wife. I told her I'm staying here tonight."

"No, you go on home. I'm fine. The doc said I'm okay. Now go."

"At least let me make you some food," he said.

Norma looked at his face. It was a kind face. She nodded. "Scramble me a couple of eggs, that'll be great."

Braden smiled. "Bacon?"

"Sounds great."

While Braden banged around in the kitchen, Norma stared at the fire behind the screen. She had fooled all of them. She was as disoriented as she had ever been in her life. She was swimming.

"I'm going to make you some biscuits, too," Braden called. "Would you like that?"

"That would be nice."

She could not remember the place she had visited well enough to describe it to herself. She only knew that she had been there. She remembered the dog. She remembered the warmth. She wished Zed could talk, could tell her something about where they'd been. She knew one thing. She would not saddle up in the morning and ride back to that place. She would not follow those tracks. She would not ride again.

Norma Snow felt warm inside. She watched the fire, the flames hovering over the alder log. She listened to the popping and the hissing. She imagined the snow falling on the cattle. She let the blankets slide down from her lap. She was warmer still. The fire grew cold.

Exposure

Benjamin Taylor's fourteen-year-old daughter was basically insane. This was what Benjamin thought as he studied the clock in the kitchen. It was nearly four thirty in the morning. On a normal night, he would have been asleep, cracking an eye at his bedside clock and enjoying the idea of another half hour of sleep. Emma had gone out, she said, with her friends Cathy and Tanya, to a movie in town, driven by Cathy's mother, she said, but Benjamin hadn't been there when she'd been picked up. He'd had a strange feeling about it when she'd called him on his cell phone. He'd been down at the stables finishing up the last of the chores. He'd asked what she was going to do about dinner and she'd said not to worry. She was fourteen and, lately, was fond of telling him not to worry. Benjamin's wife had left long ago. It had taken him six years to realize that he had been no good for her, in fact, bad for her; six years to understand that she had abandoned them as an act of survival, but still he was angry she'd gone. Now he sat and waited for his daughter. The cell phone she'd talked him into buying her went directly to her voicemail. He hated her outgoing message. She sounded like a kid trying to sound like an adult.

Three days ago at the grocery market, she had refused to get into the truck and ride home with him.

"Come on, Emma, I don't have time for this foolishness."

"I'll find my own way."

He was sitting behind the wheel, his door propped open with his foot, and she was standing at the open passenger window.

"What kind of way?" It wasn't really a question, but he felt he'd stepped badly nonetheless, entering a negotiation with a child.

"A way."

"Get in the truck."

"No."

A woman stared at them as she walked from her SUV to the grocery market door. He made brief eye contact and the woman shook her head. He didn't know whether she was disapproving of his parenting or offering commiseration for having to deal with a recalcitrant teenager. Either way, he didn't care. "Emma," he said, feeling helpless saying it.

Emma gave him and the empty passenger seat a long look and in that moment he realized that he had little leverage. His stern issuance of her name was a bluff. Just what could he do if she walked away? But she didn't walk away. For whatever reason, Benjamin wasn't questioning, Emma climbed into the truck. They headed back out to the ranch together. There he would prepare dinner. That night there would be pork chops and rice and broccoli, and she would retire to her room and sit on her phone. But before that there was the ride home.

"Are you mad at me?" Benjamin asked.

"You always ask me that," Emma said.

"I guess I do. Are you?"

"What do I always tell you?" She looked out the window at the Tasty Freeze, where she and every other teenager in Lander went at night and on weekends. It seemed like a throwback, but yet it wasn't.

"What do I always say?" she asked.

"You know, I miss your mother, too," he said, the words feeling stupid. He was already cringing at her response.

"Have you been watching talk shows again?" She laughed. "You don't miss her. She's not dead. She left us. And I can't believe you sucked me into this dumb-ass conversation."

Benjamin kept his eyes on the road. They rolled past the Target store on the edge of town and started up the hill before the descent into the valley.

A vehicle's wheels stirred the gravel of the yard. By the time Benjamin was outside, the car was just bouncing taillights and Emma was ten steps from the door. He studied the back of the car.

"Who was that?" he asked.

"Friends."

"I won't ask you if you know what time it is."

"Good."

"Have you been drinking?"

"No."

He stood in front of her on the porch. He thought better of asking to smell her breath, but he looked closely at her eyes.

"No," she repeated.

He believed her or wanted to believe her. It came to the same thing, so he did not challenge her. He took a long breath.

"Well," she said.

"Go on upstairs and get some sleep."

"That's it."

"We'll talk in the morning."

"Right."

That "right" pushed him over the edge. "Maybe you won't need much rest."

"What?"

"Since you won't be going anywhere this weekend."

"I'm supposed to go to Cathy's on Sunday," she said.

"Afraid not. Cathy won't be having guests anyway. I talked to her mother."

"You didn't."

"Around midnight a weird thing happened. I became worried about my fourteen-year-old daughter. So I called the person she said was giving her a ride. Guess what? Apparently, Cathy told her I was driving tonight."

"Shit."

"Yeah, I'm angry that you stayed out so late, but you're being grounded for lying."

Emma said nothing else, but stormed into the house and up the stairs. She did not slam her door and he knew that her failure to do so was meant to annoy him. Knowledge notwithstanding, it worked.

He sat at his kitchen table and tried to figure out not what he had done wrong but what he might do right. He decided he needed some time with his daughter, as simpleminded as that sounded, alone and away from their house. He would offer his corny attempt at some kind of remedy and she would laugh, but he would force the issue. He would make her go hiking with him. He would not go to work and he would drive her into the Winds and hike up to Burnt Lake. She would complain loudly at first and he didn't look forward to hearing that, but then it would get better. She was his daughter, so of course he loved her, but he actually liked her. He imagined that somewhere inside her she felt the same toward him.

The next morning Emma walked into the kitchen to find the counter covered with sandwiches, water bottles, and fruit. Benjamin watched her as he mixed peanuts and chocolate chips in a plastic bag.

"What's all this?" she asked.

"An outing," Benjamin said.

She looked at the mix in the bag. "Not a hike."

"Yep. I thought we'd go up to Burnt Lake. We used to go there a lot. Remember?"

"I remember."

"We need some time alone and we can get some real privacy up there."

"We have privacy here," Emma said.

"You know what I mean. Besides, here you have the phone and your computer. Smoke signals. So, go get your hiking boots on."

"You see, there's a problem."

Benjamin stared at her.

"No boots."

"I know you have hiking boots," he said.

"Yes, that's true. But I don't have hiking boots that fit. I've been doing this thing called growing, in case you haven't noticed."

"Well, we'll leave a little earlier and pick you up a pair at Lark's."

"Really, Dad?"

"Really."

"You're serious about this," she said.

"I am indeed."

Lark's was a feed and tack shop that also had a large boot department. Most were ropers and Wellingtons and paddock boots, but there were some hiking boots as well. Emma hated all of them. "I can't be seen in these things," she said. "My feet look big enough as it is."

"That's because you have big feet," Benjamin said. "Own it."

"No."

"It's not a tough hike. Just some sneaker ones will do."

She looked at the lightweight boots. "They're worse."

"You only have to wear them once."

"That's a waste of money," she said.

Benjamin mock-stared at her. "Who are you and what have you done with my daughter?"

Emma's shoulders sagged.

"Really, just once. Do the ones you have on fit?"

"I guess."

"Then we'll get those. Just humor your old man."

She started to unlace the boots.

"What are you doing?" Benjamin asked.

"I'm not wearing these things out of here. No way."

"Okay, okay."

Benjamin bought the boots and they got back into the car. Emma fiddled with the radio. "My music," she said. "Only my music."

"I wouldn't have it any other way."

What the music came to was Emma cycling through the stations. There was a preponderance of religious chatter until she got up to 100 on the dial and there was only country music she detested and at the upper end were a couple of stations playing songs in Spanish. She went through twice. She tried to turn off the radio in disgust, but managed only to turn the volume to near zero. Spanish music played softly just above the hum of the engine.

"I hate this place," she said.

"I know, honey. I'm sorry."

"Mom's in Seattle."

"How do you know that?" Benjamin asked.

"She called."

"I see." He looked out the window at the view of the mountain. "Have a good chat?"

"I guess."

"Is that where she's living now? I thought she was in Spokane."

"Was." Emma looked through the lunch pack her father had put together. "We talked about me visiting there." She opened a bag of chips, offered some to Benjamin. After he declined, she said, "It's been a year."

"Goes by fast."

"What else did you talk about?"

Emma looked out the window and said nothing.

"Remember when we used to come up here a lot?"

The girl nodded. "You tried to teach me to cast. I hated that."

"I'm sorry."

"It made me feel like you wanted a son instead of a daughter."

Benjamin swallowed hard. "I didn't know that. I just wanted to share stuff with you."

"I hated touching the fish."

"I didn't know."

He felt small and suddenly tired. "You probably won't believe me, but I was always happy to have you as a daughter. I knew you were a girl when your mother told me she was pregnant."

Emma ate a chip. "What did you bring to drink?"

"Water."

She made a face.

He thought about apologizing, but didn't.

Benjamin pulled the car off the road at the trailhead. "You know we can just go back home if you want."

Emma opened the box and looked at her boots. "We're here. Let's just do this."

"You make it sound like we're on a mission."

"Aren't we?"

"Get your shoes on." Benjamin stepped out and tightened his own laces while he waited.

Emma slammed the truck door and marched up the trail without him. He followed, caught up to her, and grabbed her arm.

"Hold on a sec," he said. "I didn't come up here to fight. I didn't bring us up here for a forced march. If you're that miserable, we can head down the mountain right now." He looked up the trail. "I don't know what you and your mother talked about. Just know that I'll do whatever will make you happy. And safe, of course."

"What if I want to move to Seattle and live with my mother?"

"Is that what she's offering?"

"What if it's what I want?"

"Of course I like having you with me. I want you with me, but I want you to be happy. Maybe you need your mother now. Or maybe you just need a break from me. I don't know." A deer bolted across the trail about thirty yards up. "I would understand that. Is that what she's said, that you can come live with her?"

"Let's hike," Emma said.

They covered the first easy mile in good time, Emma leading the way. Benjamin stopped at a mound of scat that the girl had walked past. She turned and came back to him.

"What is it?" she asked.

"Not coyote," he said. "Cougar, maybe. Pretty fresh."

Emma looked up the trail through the aspens. "What do you think?"

"We've always had cats up here," Benjamin said. "We can just head home if you want."

"No, let's go on."

Benjamin looked at the mound of scat. The ground was bone-dry and was no good for a sign. He tried to make out what might have been a track. "I wish Doc Innis was with us. Cats are nocturnal. This scat is steaming." He looked around.

"So?"

"Maybe I don't want to go on."

"Jesus, Dad."

"Are you wearing any perfume?" he asked.

"What?"

"Perfume—are you wearing any?"

"No."

"Are you having your period right now?"

"Dad!"

"Someone once told me that cats could be attracted to a menstruating woman." He had also heard that that was a myth. Still. "Are you?"

"No. Why are you so nervous? You're the one who always told me that the woods are safer than a mall."

"I don't know. You're right. I guess I'm just overprotective of my little girl."

"Give me a break." Emma started again up the trail.

Benjamin followed.

They hiked another couple of miles. The trail became steep and Emma complained about her boots.

"I'm getting a blister on my heel, I think," she said.

"Well, let's stop. I've got some moleskin." Benjamin dug into his knapsack. "We should eat our sandwiches anyway. You hungry?"

"A little."

"Get that boot off. The other feel okay?"

"I think so."

They heard a loud hiss. Both jumped.

"What was that?" Emma asked.

"I don't know," Benjamin said. They sat quietly for a few seconds. "Here, eat up. I'll get your foot squared away and we'll just head back to the car."

"What was that sound, Dad?"

"Bear, maybe. Don't worry, he's not interested in us." He put the moleskin on Emma's heel. He put her sock back on and her boot, laced it up. He patted her foot. "Just like old times," he said.

"Thanks."

"Nice view," he said.

They finished their sandwiches.

"Dad?"

"Yes, sweetie?"

"I'm sorry I stayed out so late."

"Okay. I'm over that."

"About Mom."

"Yeah?"

"You're great," she said.

"Okay."

"But I'm a girl."

Benjamin smiled at her. "I'm aware of this."

"What if I want to live with Mom for a while?"

He looked off the edge of the trail at the valley below. "I'd like to say I'd be understanding, but I can't. Your mother left us. She left you and I don't trust her now to be responsible with you."

"She's changed."

"Right." Benjamin felt small. He felt sick. This wasn't the father he wanted to be, but he could find nothing else. "We'll talk about it later."

"Right."

"You're my responsibility. I have custody of you. If she wants to all of a sudden play mommy to you, then let her prove herself to the court."

"I can go if I want."

"No, you can't. It's that simple."

Emma stepped away quickly down the slope. Benjamin moved to follow, but he landed on a round rock. What started as a skid escalated into a knee-buckling cartwheel off the side of the trail. Emma was scrambling down behind him even before he stopped rolling.

"Dad, are you all right?"

He tried to sit up, but fell back onto the slope. He knew he'd done something terrible to his right leg. His ankle was sprained, dislocated, or maybe even broken. He had to slow himself down to assess the damage. His heart was racing. His first concern was for his panicking daughter. "I'm okay," he said. "Really. I think I twisted my ankle."

"Daddy," Emma said.

He could hear in her voice that she was seeing something he had not seen yet. He looked down to see that his foot was cast off to the side at a strange angle, almost ninety degrees to his leg.

"Fuck," Benjamin said, not so much out of pain as out of anger. "Sorry."

"Does it hurt?" she asked.

"I think it's about to start hurting," he said, realizing that adrenaline was ruling the moment. "Let's get me up on the trail before it does."

Benjamin pushed and Emma pulled and they clumsily managed to get him up the hill. His ankle was erupting in pain now. He screamed.

"Is it broken?"

"I don't know," he said.

Her hands hovered over his boot.

"No, leave the boot on. I think that's the thing to do." He reached down and felt it. It was painful to touch. "It's dislocated, that's certain."

"What do we do?"

He hated hearing his child so frightened. "First thing is to relax," he said. "I'm not going to die." All he could think was that they were at least four miles from the car. "Let's see if I can stand."

"Are you kidding?"

"Help me up."

She did. He tried to put a little weight on his left foot, but it wasn't there at all. His foot flopped like a fish.

"You're going to have to drive down the mountain to get help," he said.

"What?"

"I can't walk four miles and you can't carry me."

It was then that they saw the cat on the other side of the arroyo.

"Dad, is that a cougar?"

Benjamin didn't answer.

"Daddy?"

"Yes, baby, it's a cougar. Don't panic."

"I'm not panicking."

Benjamin watched the animal disappear into the brush. The cougar looked to weigh about a hundred pounds, but still looked thin. He saw this as a bad sign. If the cat was hungry there was no telling what it might do. He couldn't let his daughter head down that trail. She was so terrified, she might break into a run at any second and so trigger the cougar's chase instinct.

"When can I panic?" she asked.

"Find me two sturdy sticks about two feet long," he said. "Let's make your old man some splints. Let's get me mobile."

"How big?"

"Strong sticks. An inch in diameter. Straight as possible."

She stood and looked around.

"Stay in sight," he said. "There should be a couple close by."

While Emma searched for the sticks, Benjamin tried to straighten out his ankle. He couldn't do it. It hurt too much. He felt like a wimp.

Emma returned with four possible splints. "What about these?" she asked.

He chose two. "These should work. Okay, now I need you to do something."

"What?"

"You're going to have to pull my foot out so I can set the splints. Just pull it. I'm going to scream, but keep pulling until it seems straight."

"I don't know," she said.

"You've got to do it. It will be all right. I'll be screaming because your dad's a big baby. Let's do it now."

She grabbed his foot and let go when he winced.

"Grab it," he said.

She did.

"On three pull hard and fast." He counted and she pulled. Benjamin tried not to scream and so made a noise that actually sounded worse. He broke into a sweat and he might have passed out for a second. The sky was too bright for his eyes for a few seconds. He collected himself. "Good, that's good."

"Good? Are you kidding me? Your leg is broken." Emma was shaking, her hands still floating over the injury.

"It's okay, baby." He sat up. He took off his shirt and belt. "Here, tear the sleeves off of this."

Benjamin positioned the sticks on either side of his ankle and secured them midcalf with his belt. "Okay, okay," he said. "Let me have a sleeve." He wrapped a sleeve tight around his ankle and foot. Just touching it made him want to vomit. To handle the pain he thought about Emma's fear. He tied the second sleeve above his knee.

"Is that it?" Emma asked.

"Help me up."

Benjamin got onto his good leg. The only good thing was that the break, if it was a break, was not compound. There was no blood. But there was plenty of pain. It quickly became clear that Emma was not going to be able to support him. "I need some bigger sticks," he said. "Crutches."

The snarl of the cougar sounded in the arroyo again.

"He's still here," Emma said.

"Big sticks." Stay on task, he told himself. "Focus," he said out loud. "Focus." He scanned the ground above him. "There!" He pointed.

Emma found the limb. "This one?"

"Yes, and find another like it. With a *Y*, just like this one."

She did, but it was a couple of inches shorter. Benjamin put the short crutch on his good side. He felt his way down the hill, keeping himself in front of Emma. He told her that if he fell he didn't want to take her out with him. And he did fall. Twice.

"Daddy, this isn't working," Emma said.

"We'll be on ground that's less steep soon. And we'll be off this hard stuff, too." The ground did level off a little, and under the canopy of trees, away from the exposed edge of the trail, the floor was more a mat of plant matter.

"See," he said. "Easy-peasy."

"I hate that expression."

"Noted."

"How is it?" she asked.

"Hurts like hell." Benjamin was sweating crazily. His T-shirt was drenched and he was starting to feel cold. He wondered if he would notice himself becoming disoriented if he started to suffer from hypothermia.

"Daddy, I'm sorry," Emma said.

"You have nothing to be sorry about," he told her. "It's your old man who has to grow up. I'm sorry."

Father and daughter stopped together on the trail. The cougar was not fifteen yards in front of them, facing them, sitting like a dog.

"So much for easy-peasy," Benjamin said.

The cat growled.

"What do we do?" Emma asked.

"We don't run, I know that," he said. He almost laughed as he considered his ankle. He was sorry to see that the animal was thin.

That meant that it was probably hungry. But that was all he could see. The lion was backlit and so there was no face to see. That made it worse, Benjamin thought.

"Dad?"

"How loud can you scream?" Benjamin asked.

"What?"

"I want you to scream as loud as you can while we walk forward, slowly forward. I'm going to scream, too, so don't be startled by how loud your old man can get."

"Really?"

"Now start screaming." And they did. Emma screamed, her voice child-high and shrill. Benjamin put a little weight on his left leg and reacted to the pain, yelled at the lion. They clung to each other and made as much noise as possible. After three small dragging steps the cougar had seen and heard enough; it ran off the trail and up the mountain.

Emma started to cry and laugh at the same time.

Benjamin started to buckle.

The girl tried to catch him and then he caught himself. "I'm okay," he told her. "Let's keep this train moving before our friend decides to come back."

"You're shivering."

"Let's go. At least it's downhill, right?"

It took them three hours to make it to the car, looking over their shoulders the whole way. Benjamin was scared to death, much of him numb. He felt he was barely lucid. His shivering was out of control. He was suffering from exposure or he was in shock. Maybe he had hit his head in the fall without knowing it and had sustained a concussion.

"You're going to have to drive," he told his daughter.

"I'm fourteen."

"I know and so I know you can do this."

He had Emma move the passenger seat all the way back. He had to be in the front to help her, to calm her, if he could. He got into the car, pushed away his crutches, and Emma closed the door. She fell in behind the wheel. She started the car and looked at her father.

"Thank god I bought an automatic," he said.

"What do I do?"

"You know what to do. First, turn up the heat."

She did.

"Now you move it to *D* and go."

"Just like that?"

"Go slow," he said. "Go slow."

Emma moved ahead.

"Good," Benjamin said. "Slow." He closed his eyes. He was starting to drift. "You can do this, sweetie."

"Daddy?"

"I'm fine. Daddy's fine. Just drive."

Wrong Lead

The big red mule backed out of the trailer as calm as anything. This was in stark contrast to the wide-eyed, on-the-muscle beast that Jake Sweeney had seen in the backyard of a trailer house just outside Dubois. He'd agreed to buy the animal without a vet check, something he'd never done before, though he was pretty good at judging equine qualities and soundness.

"I took him in," the tall woman standing next to him had said. She wore thigh-high wading boots. "There is this horse and mule rescue outfit down around Lone Pine and they brought him to me. Said he was abused."

"How so?" Jake had asked.

"Don't know. He's big and skittish. That all I've got on him. I haven't even seen him run. Not enough room here, as you can see. He's got feet like steel, the farrier said."

Jake should have backed off, found out more, but he'd fallen in love with the palomino mule at first sight.

And now here the mule was, at his place. Jake led the animal across the yard to the big pasture. Adolph, his best hand, walked ahead, opened the gate, waved the other three horses away, and closed the gate once Jake had the mule inside. Jake removed the halter. The mule stood still for a long second, then turned and broke into a wild extended trot toward the center of the pasture. The other horses trotted to and around him. He galloped away, then bucked and danced himself into a pronk. He leaped like a gazelle, all four feet together as he cleared the ground. He appeared to look around at the top of each leap.

"Wow," Adolph said.

Jake nodded. "He's pretty athletic."

"You mean scary." Though Adolph worked around horses all day, every day, he would never ride. He didn't trust horses even a little bit. He thought mules were demons.

"Why do you say that?" Jake asked.

"Well, he scares me, anyway."

"Scares me, too, Adolph." Jake thought it would be foolish not to fear a twelve-hundred-pound animal.

"That Daniels woman is down by the arena," Adolph said. "Probably has her horse out of the trailer by now."

Jake nodded. Sarah Daniels had been bringing her fancy Hanoverian to his place for several months now and he was, frankly, tired of seeing both of them. The horse was over half a ton of brainless muscle, and the woman, nice as she was, eager as she was, could not admit that she was afraid of horses. She heard what she wanted to hear, not unlike most people. Of course Jake had never accused her or even suggested she had any fear of the horse. At hopeful moments, he imagined she would break through and become the horse person she wanted to be.

Jake took a short path through the garden. When he looked at the flowers, all he could see was work that needed doing. At the other side of the house he headed down the hill to the arena. Sarah had the horse tacked and was checking the cinch as he approached.

"It's a beautiful day," Sarah said. She scratched the horse's belly. "I see you got yourself a new horse."

"Mule."

"Mule," she corrected herself. "Well, Wynn here won't pick up the turns," she said. She had a habit of abruptly getting down to business. "And he's picking up the wrong lead a lot."

Jake nodded. "Lunge him a bit and get him warmed up."

She walked over and took the lunge line and whip from the cabinet by the gate. Jake opened and closed the gate for her and she let the horse go. He kicked out and made some dust fly, then settled into a crazy trot. Jake watched his hindquarters. Sarah caught him staring.

"Something wrong?" she asked.

He shook his head and waved her off. "No, he's just loose in his caboose. Like an Arabian."

"Is that bad?" she asked.

He was sorry he'd said anything. "No, it's not bad."

"Is it good?"

"It's not anything. It's just an observation."

She reversed the horse's direction. Jake watched for a while and told her that was enough. She took the lunge line off, bridled the animal, and led him to the mounting block. She walked clockwise around the arena.

"Lazy walk," Jake called. "You're sitting, not riding."

The woman put her heels down and straightened her back. She exaggerated the straightening.

"You look like you've got a pole up your ass," he said.

She relaxed her body, but reddened slightly. She asked for a trot. She posted around twice. The horse was big, strong, but not the most beautiful mover in the world. Sarah cranked him around again.

"You see," she called out. "He's late on the turns."

As dumb as most horses are, they are never the problem, he thought. She rode past him once more.

"Tell me," he said. "What are you doing?"

The question embarrassed her. "Trotting," she said.

"No, he's trotting. What are *you* doing?"

She stopped the horse on the far side of the arena and turned to face Jake. "What are you talking about?"

"Imagine you're in your car, driving down the road," he said. "Do you look at the road or your hood ornament?"

"What?"

"Sarah, you're staring at his ears. His head is not going anyplace. It's going to be right there at the end of his neck. You're not watching the road. Listen, that animal can feel a fly land on his back. You weigh one hundred thirty pounds."

"One twenty."

"Anyway, he can feel every little thing you do up there, saddle or no saddle. He knows where you're looking and where you're not looking, but he cannot read your mind."

"What are you telling me?"

"If you're not looking for the turn, then why should he? Exaggerate it. As you come down the rail, fifteen yards before the turn, turn just your head, almost put your chin on your shoulder and see what happens."

"I'm just trying to get his head set right," she said.

"Forget that. Just try what I said."

Sarah started the horse. She did what Jake had suggested and the horse smoothly moved into the turns.

"How's that?" he asked.

"That feels great."

"You don't have to move your head so much. He can feel it all through your seat. Keep going."

They finished the session and Jake left Sarah with her horse at the wash rack. He walked back to the pasture gate and watched the new mule. He had settled down and was grazing by the far fence.

Jake went inside for a cup of tea. He drank while he sat on his front porch. Beyond his garden, he could see the pasture and the mule. He looked at his poor, neglected roses. He could see the pale masses of aphids crowding the blooms from twenty paces. Sitting out here with tea seemed the only civilized thing he did anymore. He hardly ever listened to music, though he heard tunes in his head from time to time. He seldom read for pleasure these days, though he would buy an occasional book and add it to his stack. It wasn't as if he had been devastated by his wife's leaving or even by the fact that she had left him for another man. He was, in fact, in a way, quite relieved. They had both been unhappy, miserable, in fact, and he had been either too strong or too weak to end it, telling himself every day

that he could make it right. In truth he knew it was the latter, that he
was weak. The sad part was he'd become comfortable with the un-
happiness, perhaps the unhealthiest of states. He was lonelier since
she'd left, perhaps messier, in some ways at loose ends, but he was
unquestionably happier. He was thankful to his ex-wife for that. At
least she'd had the strength to leave. He did not feel the sort of shame
or embarrassment his family and friends seemed to think he felt or
maybe believed he ought to feel. He kept up with his work, his animals, but apparently not his garden.

"Jake," Sarah greeted him from the bottom of the porch steps. She
was wet from hosing down the horse.

"Packed up?"

"I put him in the round pen."

"That's fine," he said.

She looked around the garden. "This is a great garden. I've always
loved your roses."

"I'm glad you do. Apparently I'm not loving them enough. I've got
deadheading to do, powdery mildew, aphids."

"You're awfully hard on yourself," she said. She sniffed a wide-
open lavender bloom.

"That's a Whisky Mac," Jake said. "It's the only hybrid tea in the
place. That one smells just wonderful."

"What's wrong with hybrid tea roses?"

"Just a prejudice," Jake said. "Like some people don't like Appaloosas. I don't like hybrid teas. You know why god gave Indians
Appaloosas, don't you?"

Sarah shook her head.

"He did it so they would be plenty good and mad by the time they
rode into battle."

She smiled.

"I know it's not the best joke. Sort of politically incorrect, I guess."
He paused. "Pardon my manners. Would you like a cup of tea?"

"That sounds nice, thank you."

Jake left her on the porch and walked through his living room and into the kitchen. He put on the water and stood waiting. He glanced around. His ex-wife was now two years gone and still the place looked like her. He wondered briefly what the ranch house of a single man should look like. Army surplus forks and knives that didn't match. Lots of leather, chairs and sofa. A Lucite table with barbed wire suspended inside it. He'd seen one once. The kettle called.

Back on the porch he found Sarah sitting on the top step. He sat beside her, handed her the mug. "It's a warm day. Maybe I should have offered you something cold."

"It's never too warm for tea," she said.

Jake looked at the hills beyond the pasture again.

She looked where he looked. "Not too shabby," she said.

"I like it."

"So, why do you like mules so much?" Sarah asked.

Jake sipped his tea. "They're smart. I like them because they're really smart. That trait makes them a challenge to train."

"I thought they were stubborn."

"That's because they're smart. You tell a horse to walk off a cliff, off he goes. You tell a mule to do the same thing and he'll just look at you like you're a fool. More, he'll never listen to another thing you say."

"So, what happened to your wife?"

Jake stared ahead. "That's direct."

"Sorry. It a nervous tic."

"I don't mind," he said. "It's refreshing. She left me."

"Why?"

He nearly chuckled. "Because I wasn't a very attentive husband. It seems I'm attentive in many ways to all sorts of things and not in some others. She left me because I was a lousy husband."

"That's redundant."

"Perhaps." Jake finished his tea and set down his mug. "So, what do you do when you're not hauling that beast around and riding?"

"That's the first question you have ever asked me that didn't involve horses and it kind of did," she said.

"I like horses."

"I used to be a middle school teacher," she said. "I got laid off. Laid off. Sounds like it should feel good."

"And your husband?"

"How do you know I have a husband?"

"Wife? Partner? Associate? I don't know. Somehow I imagined you attached to someone."

"Is that a good thing or a bad thing?" she asked.

"Neither. A lazy assumption."

"Construction. My mister is in construction." She looked at her tea. "Do you think I'll ever be a good rider?"

Jake shrugged. "What do you mean by good rider?"

Sarah didn't like his answer; it was not the one she was looking for. He could tell by the way her gaze did not rise from her tea. Finally she looked up and across the pasture.

Jake glanced at his watch, measured his time for the day. "Come on, let's go for a ride," he said.

"What?"

"Let's saddle up and pop some brush. A trail ride."

"Wynn is no good on trails."

"Sure he is. Let's go."

Jake rode a sturdy quarter horse he called Trotsky. He was a good hand shorter than Sarah's big Hanoverian. They rode through the tractorway between the pastures toward the hills. The horses and the mule raised their heads to watch, then went back to grazing. They started up the slope.

"Last time I took this guy on a trail ride he balked at every little thing," Sarah said.

"Well, it's a different day. If he balks, he balks."

She nodded.

"If it rains, it rains," Jake said. "Has he ever run away with you?"

"No." But the question unnerved her.

"That's a good thing."

They crested the ridge and looked down a little coulee. Trotsky sneezed. "Allergies," Jake said.

"It's beautiful."

The trail was clear to see from where they stood. It meandered through low brush, disappeared into the trees at streamside, then showed itself again on the far side of the water and climbed steeply up the next ridge.

"So, what do you see?" Jake asked.

"The creek," she said. "Wynn doesn't like water."

"You just sprayed him with a hose."

"That kind of water. He hates to cross water."

Jake stared at the creek with her for a few seconds. "How deep do you reckon that stream is?"

"I don't know."

"As high as my knee?"

"Not that high."

"So, you mean to tell me that if there was a hill of carrots on the other side of that water, your horse wouldn't cross it?"

"No."

"He could and he would."

"Okay."

"Where are we looking to go?" He didn't wait for the answer to his rhetorical question. "We're going to the top of that next ridge."

"Okay."

"We're not going to the edge of the creek. We're not going to the downed log on the other side. I can sit here and find obstacles all day. And if I find them, so will the horse."

"I understand."

"I'm sitting on a behemoth with a brain the size of a Brazil nut. He can only process so much. All he needs to know is that I'm going over there." He pointed with his chin.

"That's easy to say," Sarah said.

"True enough."

He led the way down the trail. Sarah's horse was of course more comfortable with another horse in front of him. Some clouds passed in front of the sun. They got into the trees and Jake pulled up ten or so yards from the creek.

"Let's go around that way," he said.

"Why?"

"Snake on a rock."

Though she did not see the snake, Sarah's body tensed up and the horse felt it. The Hanoverian hopped and kept hopping. Sarah lost one stirrup and nearly lost her balance. Jake watched her. He did nothing. There was nothing to do. She regained control of the horse.

"Let's go," he said, without pause, without acknowledging what had just happened.

Twenty yards downstream they crossed the water without incident. Jake still said nothing, but inside he was yelling at himself. He had been frightened that Sarah was going to have a wreck. Having a wreck was not a bad thing in itself, but it was a bad place to have one. He was content to let her think he thought nothing had happened. Her horse hopped a step and moved slightly to the side, but that was it.

They finished the ride without mishap. Wynn crossed the creek again on the way back. Sarah seemed better for the time on the trail. Jake helped her load her horse and watched her trailer bounce away down his drive.

He helped Adolph with the feeding and checking of the paddocks, then stood with him as he fell in behind the wheel of his truck.

"Out riding with the ladies," Adolph said.

"I'm a player, what can I say."

Adolph laughed.

"Is she nice?"

"I just took her out for a lesson."

"A lesson," Adolph repeated. "How much did she pay you?"

"You should be going," Jake said.

"I'll be late tomorrow. Gotta take my cat to the vet."

Jake nodded.

In his kitchen he fried a steak the way he knew he was not supposed to and sat alone at his table to eat. He imagined he was in-
dulging in very patient suicide. He thought about the day. He didn't
know what had gotten into him. When Sarah had said her horse was
spooked on trails, he should have listened. It wasn't the horse's fault,
what had happened. It wasn't Sarah's fault, nervous as she was. It
was his. He'd been cocky and for that there was no excuse. He was
confused by it. Perhaps he was lonelier than he imagined and so just
showing off for the attention of a woman. He'd talked too much and
had not thought enough. Luckily, nothing bad had happened. It was
a bad day when you had to depend on luck.

Clouds crept in during the night and the pouring rain was a surprise in the morning. He fed the pastured animals under the sheds.
He took the shovel and dug some channels to let water run out of the
paddocks. The horses always managed to mound the dirt up under
the pipe corrals and so the water would stand. He then went back inside to feed himself. He wanted to take the new mule out, lunge him
a bit, but even if the rain let up, the round pen and the arena would
be too muddy. It wasn't possible anyway; the rain came harder. He
listened to it on his roof. He ate his eggs and bacon, drank his coffee, and read the paper. He picked up a book he'd recently purchased
at a discount bookstore. It was about Pickett's Charge at Gettysburg.
Jake had never had much interest in the Civil War, but he thought
he might as well develop one. He had just understood the landscape
of the battefield when the phone rang.

It was Sarah Daniels. "I'm sorry to call you," she began.

"That's not the best icebreaker I've heard," he said.

"I know you're busy."

"It's fine. I don't know what it's doing at your house, but it's pouring over here. So, I'm not doing much."

"It's pouring here, too."

"What can I do for you?"

"I need to talk to you."

"Okay, shoot."

"Not on the phone," she said.

"Pardon?"

"Will you meet me?"

"Sarah?"

"I just need to talk."

Jake looked out the window at the rain that was not letting up.

"I'm sorry. I shouldn't have called."

"No, no, it's okay. Sure, you can come over."

"No, I want you to come meet me at the Big Boy."

"Bob's Big Boy?"

"Yes."

"Sarah, I don't know."

"I'll treat you to an early lunch."

Jake looked at the clock. It was ten. "Eleven okay?"

Jake hung up. He felt uneasy. He decided to combine the trip with a stop at the vet supply store so he could pick up deworming paste. Maybe he'd step into the tack store beside it and look at the saddles he would never buy.

At Bob's Big Boy Jake sat in his pickup and watched the sun come out. He wanted to be at home instead, but things still needed more than a few hours to dry out. Later that afternoon maybe he could at least take the mule out for a walk. He glanced at his rearview mirror and saw Sarah enter the restaurant.

Inside, he stepped past the hostess's station and the glass case full of big pies and cakes, saw Sarah seated in a booth by the window. He walked over and fell onto the bench opposite her.

"Sarah."

"Thank you for coming." She sipped her water.

"This is strange, you know?" Jake said.

"I know. I'm sorry."

"So, what's up?"

The waitress came by. Jake picked up the menu and handed it to her. "Burger, fries, coffee. Thank you, ma'am."

"Just a salad," Sarah said. "And iced tea."

The waitress left.

Sarah looked around the room and that made Jake glance around. He suddenly felt furtive and he didn't like it.

"Sarah?"

"You helped me a lot the other day."

"I'm glad to hear that."

"Not just with the horse. All that talk about not staring at the horse's head, about looking ahead to where I'm going and not seeing obstacles. I understood what you were saying."

"I see," he said. "That's good, right?" Jake looked at the now very sunny day. "And?"

Sarah sat back against the cloth-covered booth, seemed to smile slightly as she looked out the window. "I want to know something, Jake. Do you find me attractive?"

The waitress returned with the tea and coffee.

"Thank you, ma'am," Jake said.

The waitress left.

Jake took the interruption as a chance to change the subject. "Every now and then you're going to have a breakthrough with horses. I've been riding for forty years and it still happens."

"Do you find me attractive?"

"Sarah, what's this all about?"

"Answer the question."

"I'm uncomfortable with the question."

"Why?"

"I just don't want to answer the question." Jake wanted to get up and leave. And he also wanted to stay. "You're a married woman." His voice was soft, quiet. He tried to avoid whispering. He thought whispering would make him feel like he was up to something.

"Do . . . you . . . find me attractive?"

"Yes."

"See, that wasn't difficult," she said.

"Is that why I'm here? To tell you that you're pretty?"

"No."

"I just wanted to thank you," she said.

"For what? Listen, I'm flattered and I hope that I'm not letting some male fantasy make me think you're coming on to me, but that's what I'm thinking."

"I'm not coming on to you. I'm thanking you."

"It sure feels like you're coming on to me," he said.

"You convinced me to leave my husband."

The waitress delivered the food, but Jake didn't look away from Sarah. "Ketchup?" the waitress asked. "Ketchup?"

"No, thank you," Jake said without looking at her.

The woman left.

"I don't want to hear that," he said. "About your husband." He looked at his food. He put some money on the table. "Listen, thanks for inviting me out, but I've got to go."

"What are you so afraid of?" she asked.

"I've got to go." He started to stand, but stopped. "I appreciate that you've got troubles. I hope you find what you want. But I don't know you, Sarah. We're not close friends. All I wanted was for your horse to cross the creek."

"I know, but—"

"For your horse to cross the creek," he repeated. "Okay, I'm going now." He gained his feet and walked out.

Things were fairly dried out by the time Jake arrived home. He stepped into his mudroom and changed into his paddock boots, then went straight for the mule. He hadn't eaten and he was hungry, but he needed to work an animal. The mule was not eager to come to him, so he had to angle him off until he had him in a corner to halter him. He led him out and to the cross ties in the barn. The mule stepped nervously, but calmed under the currycomb.

Adolph pulled his pickup into the yard and came into the barn. "I thought it was going to rain all day," he said.

"Seemed like it." Jake rubbed the mule's belly with the comb and found he liked it. "I thought we'd start worming everybody."

"I'll get the list."

Jake had found a list was necessary when giving the deworming paste. One of his donkeys liked the paste so much she'd crowd in to get a second dose.

"Anybody else showing up today?" Jake asked.

"Juan went to get a new valve for the donkey's water trough."

"Again?"

"They tear things up."

"Don't forget the list," Jake said.

"You okay?" Adolph asked.

Jake tossed the currycomb down and picked up a stiff-bristled brush. "Yeah, I'm fine. Why?"

"I'll get the list."

"Sounds good. The medicine is on the front seat of my pickup. I'm going to lunge this guy a bit and I'll join you."

Adolph walked away. Jake realized he'd repeated himself and called out, "And don't forget the list."

"Yeah, the list."

Jake cleaned out the mule's hooves. He was a bit unwilling to lift his left hind foot and so Jake made a mental note to watch that side during the exercise. He took him out of the cross ties and to the arena. It usually dried faster than the round pen. The mule ran like a fool clockwise around him about five times until he settled down to a long trot. He let him go for a while without asking for anything. He moved well and Jake could see no unevenness or problem with his tracking. He slowed him, then had him walk. He had a nice walk. Jake stopped him, pulled him close, and scratched his neck. He turned him and sent him off into a walk the other way. He asked for a trot and the mule gave it to him. He asked for a canter and there it was, correct lead and everything. That was good for a first time out, he thought. Always end on a good note. Always end with compliance. He reeled him in and praised him. The mule tried to rub his big head against Jake's jacket, but Jake wouldn't let him. He scratched the animal's nose with his hand.

Jake brushed the mule down, cleaned his hooves again, and put him back in the pasture. His phone rang. He walked over and answered the extension just inside the barn.

"This Jake Sweeney?"

"Yes."

"This is Clark Daniels."

"Yes?"

"Sarah's husband."

"I see."

"I want to come by and talk to you," the man said.

"Listen, I'm really busy and I don't like being involved in other people's business," Jake told him.

"Just for a few minutes."

Jake looked at the near-cloudless sky. It was a pale cerulean, looked like it hadn't rained and like it never would again. "What's this all about? I don't want to get mixed up in—"

"I'll be there in thirty minutes." The man hung up.

Jake set the receiver gently back into its cradle and stood for a few seconds. "Adolph!" he called out.

Adolph came from the far side of the paddocks.

"How many more to do?" Jake asked.

"I'm half-done."

"We'll finish them tomorrow. You go on home."

"What? It's early."

"It's fine. Just head on. I'll take care of the feed and we can finish up the worming tomorrow."

"You're the boss."

The hills were quiet. The road was quiet. So was the ranch. A hawk circled over the far field. Jake walked through his garden, paused at the Whisky Mac hybrid tea that Sarah had admired. He did not lean over to sniff it. The woman's husband was on his way to Jake's house and Jake had no idea what to expect, what to do. Did the man have the idea that his wife was having an affair with Jake? If Daniels did think that, what could Jake say that he would believe? Had the man seen Jake and Sarah at Bob's Big Boy? He laughed to himself, felt the hollowness in his gut, and wished he had eaten that burger. He would wait for the man and handle what developed. Fretting wasn't going to change anything.

Jake was blasting his roses with a narrow spray from the hose to remove aphids when the fancy Dodge pickup with the shiny bed-cover came up the drive. He turned off the water and walked to the truck. A tall man with a belly got out from behind the wheel.

"Mr. Daniels," Jake said.

"Clark," the man said and reached out to shake.

Jake took his hand.

"Thanks for your time."

Jake nodded. "What can I do for you?"

"I want to know about you and my wife."

Jake bristled at the sound of that, but didn't detect any malice. If anything the man seemed as confused as Jake. "There's nothing to tell," he said. "She brings her horse over here and I watch her ride occasionally."

"I know that," Daniels said.

"You know what?" Jake asked.

"That she comes over here. You know, she spends all of her time with that damn horse. That's all she ever talks about. Then the other night she started talking about you."

They were standing in Jake's yard. Jake thought it felt strange to be standing outside talking like this.

"She told me you opened her eyes."

"I've done a lot of things in my so-called life, but I've never opened anybody's eyes."

"She claims that a trail ride with you gave her the courage she needed to let me go."

"She said that, did she?"

"She did."

"You realize that there's nothing between your wife and me. Not just romantically; we're not even friends."

"I believe that," Daniels said, but Jake didn't quite buy it. "I just want to know what you said to her."

"Listen, I don't know what I said to her. Probably the same thing I say to her every time I watch her ride her horse, to stop staring at his head and watch where she's going."

"That's it?"

Jake looked at the big truck and then at the man for the first time. He was dressed sharply; one might have called him a dandy. His suede boots looked expensive. His shirt was starched. His trousers were creased. His hairline receded somewhat. He had large hands, but they were soft.

"She really loves all this horse shit," Daniels said, then laughed at his accidental joke.

"She does," Jake agreed. "She wants to be good at it."

"Is she?"

"She's afraid of horses."

The man blew out a breath. "She's afraid of a lot."

"Don't get me wrong," Jake said. "It makes sense to be scared of horses. They're half a ton of dynamite waiting to go off."

"What are you saying?"

"I'm not saying anything. Why does every-fucking-body think I'm trying to say more than I am? I'm saying that a horse can be dangerous. You can't forget that. Your wife knows that."

"Why does she like it then?"

"I can't tell you that," Jake said.

"Why do you like it?"

"I like horses. They're honest. I haven't had one cheat me or lie to me or betray me yet. And they allow me to ride them. Have you ever been on a horse?"

"No."

Jake looked at the man, then around the pasture at the hills. "How much time do you have?"

"Why?"

"You got half an hour?"

"Okay."

Jake brought Trotsky out of the pasture and led him to the hitching post outside his kitchen door. He gave the gelding's back a quick brushing and cleaned out his hooves.

"How long have you been doing this?" Daniels asked.

"Most of my life," Jake said. He left the man standing by the horse and grabbed a big roper's saddle that he hardly used anymore. It had a deep seat and a high cantle, seemed to suck a rider in. He put the saddle on Trotsky's back and reached beneath him for the cinch.

"What are you doing?" the man finally asked.

"I'm saddling a horse," Jake said.

"I can see that. Why?"

"You're going to ride him."

"No, I'm not."

"Listen, I don't know you or your wife, but here you are at my house looking for answers. You asked me why she loves horses. I'm going to see if this helps you understand. I can't make you get on this beast. I can't do that any more than I can make this giant animal do something he doesn't want to do."

Daniels looked at his truck like he wanted to jump in it and drive off down the road.

"Come on. Two walks around an enclosed arena and you'll know just a little more than you knew before you came here. Maybe."

Jake didn't wait for a reply. He walked the horse away from the post and toward the arena. Daniels followed. In the arena, Jake took the horse to the mounting block. He looked at Daniels.

"What?"

"Get on. Step up there and throw your leg over."

Daniels did. Jake handed him the reins. "You want to go left, you touch the right side of his neck with the reins. Right, the left side."

"I don't know about this."

"Relax. Nice shoes, by the way."

"How do I make him go?"

"Say, 'Walk on.'"

"Walk on."

Trotsky did. He hung his head and walked like he thought he was carrying a kid. He brought the man all the way around. Jake waved him on.

A car came into the yard. It was Sarah Daniels. She parked near her husband's truck and walked down the slope to the arena. Jake turned and walked past her on his way to his house. He didn't say anything. He didn't look at her. He just let her walk down to the arena.

Jake went back to his roses. Damn aphids.

The Day Comes

"All I know is them cows didn't shoot themselves." Hugh Rakes walked around to the other side of the corral. The steers were back-to-back and head to tail in the mud. It was raining hard. The damage to their heads was unmistakable. Some large-caliber weapon had done it.

Sheriff Howard Gunther, Rakes's closest neighbor, snapped a few photos of the dead cows and shook his head. The early evening was cold and he wished he were at home.

"I was up clearing out that damn culvert. Didn't hear a fucking thing." Rakes took his hat off, slapped the rain off it, and put it back on.

"This one's been shot twice," Gunther said.

"Yeah. He wasn't quite dead when I found them and I had to finish the job. Son of a bitch. If I find the son of a bitch that did this I'm going to—"

"We don't need talk like that, Hugh. I know you're upset. I wish I could tell you I had some idea." Gunther stepped away and looked at the soaked dirt-and-gravel yard. "Well, let's circle our way away from the pen and see if we can find some shell casings in this mess."

"This one is mine," Rakes said, handing the spent round to the sheriff. "I picked it up for you."

Gunther took it and put it in his pocket. It helped to have it only because he wouldn't have to find it himself. They found nothing. "So, he picked up his brass. That the way you see it?"

"Must have."

Gunther put away his camera and frowned at the rain. "At least your insurance will take care of it. It will take care of your loss, won't it?"

Rakes nodded, rubbed his hand through his hair.

Gunther watched him for a bit.

"Goddamn," Rakes said.

"I'll be off now," Gunther said.

"Yeah, all right."

Gunther got into his rig. He sat there for a minute watching the worn wipers streak the windshield. He then drove the mile to his house. He walked into the kitchen and found his wife sitting at the table writing out checks to pay the bills.

"Where have you been?" she asked.

"I was over at Rakes's place. He was showing me his cows that were mysteriously murdered."

"What?"

"I almost believed him until he claimed he was cleaning out the old culvert. County cleaned that out last month."

"Why would he shoot his own animals?" Karen asked.

"Insurance. They weren't his best animals. I could see that he'd switched ear tags. Probably would have done that anyway. He's up there now dressing out those steers and saving what meat he can."

"What are you going to do?"

Gunther shrugged. "Nothing. It's fraud either way. The insurance agent will come around and I will confirm that the stock were shot and that will be it. I hate this fucking job." He poured himself a cup of coffee. "You want some more?"

Karen shook her head no.

"Don't get me wrong, I like that nothing ever happens around here. I hate that all I do is put people I know in lockup for DUI. Remember that song 'Lineman for the County'? Well, that job's a hell of a lot more interesting than mine."

"But you've got me," Karen said.

Gunther leaned over and kissed her forehead. "That is true, isn't it? I don't know how it happened, but it's true."

The next morning Gunther left his wife asleep in the bed, dressed, and left for his office. He stopped on the way and walked into the Square Wheel Diner. It had been called the Wagon Wheel, but so much of the business now came from the RV park across the road that the owner changed the name. The RVers could walk over and at once identify with the reference to having to wait for their tires to warm up on the road on cold mornings before assuming any roundness. The locals came in, too, and Gunther sat at a table with Dorothy Wise and Danny Denton.

"I'll start with some coffee, ma'am," Gunther told the waitress. "A little milk with that."

"So," Wise said.

"So? So what?" Gunther looked at the menu, though he knew it by heart.

"Why bother looking at that?" Denton said. "You order the same thing every time. Hell, they're back there cooking it right now."

"I could change."

"So, are you going to let him get away with it?"

"Let who get away with what?"

"Rakes," Wise said. She was a big woman, broad shouldered, but not fat. She lived alone on her family spread and raised cattle.

"Oh, that."

"Yeah, that," she said. "You know he shot those beefs."

"And I can't prove it."

"He's gonna get all of our insurance rates jacked up," Wise said.

"That's for sure," Denton said. Denton was an accountant and had an office attached to his home in town.

"You don't have stock," Gunther said to Denton.

"No, but I know insurance companies, and they use any excuse at all to raise rates."

"So, what are you going to do?"

"What can I do? He called me out on a rainy day and told me some-body shot his animals. His yard was like a hogs' pen in that rain, nothing but slop. No footprints, no tire tracks. Just two dead steers and his word."

"But you know he did it," Wise said.

"I think, Dorothy. It's up to the insurance company. I'll insinuate what I think, but I can't make any accusations. I mean, what if he's telling the truth?"

"Ha," Wise said.

"What she said," from Denton.

The waitress brought Gunther his oatmeal and wheat toast. He looked up at her face.

"Were you going to order something different?" she asked.

"Thank you," Gunther said. The waitress left and Daniel returned his attention to Wise. "What would you do?"

Wise looked at her coffee. "I don't get paid to do your job."

"I see." Gunther pointed his spoon at Denton.

"Careful where you point that," Denton said.

Gunther put the spoon back in his oatmeal. "What about you? Any ideas?"

"I guess not."

"You two are a lot of help." He drank some coffee. "I'm going to eat my breakfast, then I'm going to go write up my murder report on two beefs, and then I'm going to fill out my usual nothing-happened-this-week report and send it to the state of Wyoming to be filed with the rest of such reports."

"You need a vacation," Denton said.

"From what?" Gunther ate a bit of oatmeal and put down his spoon. He looked out the window at the RV park across the road. "Hell, those RVers don't cause any trouble, 'cause they're all eighty years old." He looked at his friends. "Well, I'm going home to tend to my wife's horse's hooves."

"You're not going to the office?" Wise asked.

"How can I put this?" Gunther said. "Fuck the office."

"Howard," Wise said.

"See you later."

Gunther, in fact, did not go to his office. He did call his secretary, Grace, and tell her he wouldn't be there; there was no point in worrying an old woman and even less reason to get her mad at him. But he didn't drive home. Instead he drove up into the mountains to an abandoned fishing and hunting lodge. The building had never been completed. It had hardly been started. There was some of the large foundation dug, but the rest had only been staked and strung. The blue plastic string was gone now except for where the ends had been tied. The people who had started it ran into legal trouble, then investor trouble, and bailed. He fantasized about buying the property and finishing the project himself, but he knew that wouldn't happen.

He wondered if he was really that unhappy with his job. He'd run for office because he could, because he was retired from the Marines and thought the job would be easy. And in fact it was. It was too easy. It was boring. He was fifty and bored. He had a nice wife who was perhaps more capable than he was in more ways. He had a teenage daughter who pretended to like him on occasion. He had a twenty-five-year-old son who lived in Denver who never bothered to pretend. Here he was shirking his duties to daydream on a mountain and not a great daydream at that, it having drifted rather seamlessly into self-pity.

He was depressed. He was not simply sad. He wasn't simply bored. He felt a weight on his chest that made him want to cry. Sometimes in the night he did. He would discover himself crying and that discovery worked as fuel for more tears. He was embarrassed by it, then embarrassed for feeling embarrassed. His wife would understand, he thought. If she knew he was crying she would hold him, stroke his head, and make soothing sounds, but he didn't want that. He hated feeling so low and yet could not deny a desire to wallow in it. He felt selfish. He felt small and he felt more lost than he had ever felt in his life. He looked at the unfinished foundation and saw himself, once strung taut, now just a mere suggestion of defined space.

Gunther arrived home to find his daughter and wife sitting on the porch. Their faces were blank, somewhat sour, showing fear perhaps. He walked toward the porch, his eyes asking, "What?"

"Tell him," Karen said.

The girl looked at the sky.

"Tell him," Karen repeated.

"What is it, Sarah?" Gunther asked. He was lately always out of the loop, but now he felt high tension. Karen was frightened as well as angry. "What's going on here?"

"I'm pregnant," Sarah said, flatly.

Gunther stepped away, turned, and sat on the first step. He understood the words and yet they made no sense. He looked at his little girl. He wasn't angry. He was confused.

"Did you hear your daughter?" Karen asked.

He said nothing.

"Did you hear her?"

"I heard." He didn't know where to go with this news. He might have been angry. He might have been scared. He didn't know. He decided to not be angry and so put his hand up. "Come here, Sarah," he said. He felt her hand find his and led her around to sit beside him, put his arm around her.

"Are you scared?"

The girl started crying.

"It's okay," he told her. "Everything will be okay." He thought about the father. He had no idea who he was and felt himself getting angry. He stopped. His daughter was terrified. He looked up at his wife.

"Ask her who the father is," she said. Karen was angry.

"Not now, Karen."

Karen walked into the house.

"I'm sorry, Daddy."

Gunther said nothing.

"Danny is the father," the girl said.

"Does he know?"

"I told him. He's terrified you're going to shoot him."

"I might." He looked at the graying sky. "You can tell him that I'm not going to shoot him."

"He says he'll marry me."

"That's just stupid," Gunther said. "You're only seventeen. Even if you were nineteen, that would be stupid. He's what? Eighteen? You don't need two children to take care of."

"I want to go to Denver," Sarah said.

"Do you?"

"Yes."

"I want you to think about this hard. I'm not going to tell you what to do, but I want you to think it through real good."

"Okay."

"You think I should talk to Danny?" he asked.

"I wish you wouldn't," Sarah said.

"Well, I'm going to see him around. I reckon I ought to talk to him just a little bit, don't you think? I'm not going to scare him. I promise." It was a promise Gunther meant, but knew it would be difficult to keep. He felt strangely good about himself for the measured calm of his reaction, felt like he was being a good father. He realized what a rare feeling that was for him. "I'll take you to Denver if you want. Just tell me when."

The girl was crying hard now. He held her.

Karen was sitting up in bed pretending to read a fat novel when Gunther came into the room. He walked over to their bedroom window and looked out at the yard below.

"Tell me how could this happen?" she said. "How could she let something like this happen?"

"It happened," he said.

"What are you going to do about it?"

"I'm going to take care of our daughter. Just like you. That's really all we can do."

"And about the boy, what are you going to do about the boy?" Karen closed her book and tossed it onto the rug at her bedside. "She's seventeen. He's eighteen. Isn't that statutory rape?"

Gunther sat on the bed and put his hand on Karen's foot. She pulled it away. "What will arresting that boy do for Sarah? It will tear her up. That Danny's not a bad kid. I don't like him much, but he's not a bad kid. What will that do to him? To his parents? What will it do to us?"

"Why are you all of a sudden Mr. Calm?"

"I don't know." Gunther looked across the room and out the window. "Is that snow?" He walked over to look out. There was a flurry, the snow moving harmlessly, the wind hardly a bother.

He turned to see that Karen had picked up and opened her book. She pretended to read again. It was clear she was not going to look at him.

Gunther went downstairs and sat alone in the kitchen, watched the snow turn serious. The truth was that Gunther did feel windless. He felt unusually calm and he wasn't sure it felt good, though he was pleased with how he was handling the situation with his daughter. He held his hand out, like a gunfighter in a movie, to check his steadiness. His hand did not quiver. He checked his pulse. Fifty. It had never been fifty. He wanted to be anxious about his newfound serenity, but instead he grew even more relaxed. The irony was not lost on him and in fact played out as being strange and slightly amusing.

He left his house, moving toward his office. At the crossroads outside town he came upon his young deputy, Marty Hawn. He was leaning against his patrol car, smoking a cigarette.

"I thought you were giving those up," Gunther said.

"Seems kinda silly having to smoke out in the snow like this," the young man said.

"Everything okay?"

"So far. How about with you?"

Gunther stared out through his windshield and wondered what a truthful answer might sound like. "It's been an interesting day," he said.

Marty offered a quizzical look. He was only twenty-one and didn't look that old, a big kid who had excelled in high school football, but wasn't good enough for a college scholarship. He liked astronomy.

"Come by the station after your rounds. We'll take Grace out and grab some coffee," Gunther said.

"I'd like that."

His cell phone rang and he answered it. It was Grace. "Are you coming in to the office?"

"I suppose I should."

"Where are you now?" she asked.

"With Marty at the Shell station. What's up?"

"Apparently Gilly White is out plowing the road in front of his house."

Gunther looked at the hills and the roads. "But the snow's not even on the ground yet."

Grace said nothing.

"I'm heading over there now."

"What is it?" Marty asked.

"Gilly White's acting crazy again."

"You want me to go over there?"

Gunther shook his head. "I'll see to it. You finished your shift."

By the time Gunther arrived at Gilly White's place, snow was beginning to stick to the ground. White's tractor was parked halfway off the road, the snowplow blade down and lifting the front end just a bit. The dirt road was a mess, deep gouges and wounds that promised to become fantastically problematic once the lane was wet from rain or melting snow. Gunther got out of his truck and walked over to where White sat on the running board of his tractor.

"Been drinking?" Gunther asked.

"You can tell?"

"A guess."

Gilly White was holding a pistol in his left hand. He was missing the middle finger of his right. Gunther had never asked him how he lost it. Gunther didn't like the gun there, didn't like them much anywhere. He was not armed. His pistol was in his glove box. He didn't like wearing it.

"Yeah, I been drinking," White said.

Gunther looked at the tractor and road. "You did quite a number on the road there."

"Needed plowing."

"Done?"

"Out of gas," White said. He traced the top of the barrel of the pistol with his right index finger.

Gunther slowly pulled his mobile phone from his pocket. He called his office. "Grace, I'm over at the White place. Yes, everything is all right. The tractor's out of gas in the road."

"You want me to send Horace with his tow truck?"

"Yeah, send Marty out here with some gas," Gunther said.

"I understand," Grace said. "Right away."

Gunther put his phone away. He looked up at the sky. "You were right to start plowing. This is going to be a big storm."

"Yeah, a real blizzard."

Gunther looked back at White's house. It was set some fifty yards off the road, down a straight drive. The front door of the house was open. No smoke came from the chimney. "Your family at home?"

"Oh, yeah," White said.

"How are they doing?"

"You know."

"Tell me, Gilly. How are they?"

"You ever play Xbox?"

"What?"

"Xbox."

"No. What's that?"

"A video game."

Gunther nodded. "I don't know much about that stuff. How old is your son now? Is he six yet?"

"Not yet."

"You want to wait here for the gas? I think I'll go say hello to Kate. What's your boy's name?"

"David."

"And David. You going to be okay here?"

White nodded.

Gunther didn't like turning his back on the man, but he had to get to the house. As he approached he was struck by the stillness, the coldness of it. He felt cold inside. He wanted Marty to be there already. As soon as he stepped through the door he called Grace.

"Where's Marty?"

"Ten minutes away."

"Tell him to make it five."

"What's going on?"

"Tell Marty I'm in the house. Tell him to be ready."

"Howard."

"Tell him to hurry, Grace. I need him here now."

He closed his phone. The house was freezing. He called out for Kate White, but no one answered. He looked out the front window just as Gilly White gained his feet and turned to start for the house.

Gunther ran up the stairs. He saw the boy first. He was lying on a round carpet in the hallway. There was no need to check for signs of life. There was blood everywhere. The rug was soaked. The small body was twisted in an angle that only death would allow. He walked past the boy and into the front bedroom. The woman was on her back on the bed, her light-blue pajama top soaked with blood. Gunther checked for a pulse while he looked out the window to see White some fifteen yards from the house. The woman was just alive, but wouldn't be for long. She was wide open. Gunther pushed the sheet over and into her wound.

Gunther looked out the window and saw that Marty was just parking behind his rig on the road. He ran back down the stairs and into the kitchen. He sat at the table and tried to figure out what to do. He looked around the room for a weapon, but decided a big knife might just make things worse. He could not shake what he had just seen from his mind. He thought about his daughter. He thought about her baby, her decision, being a grandfather perhaps. His wife was home waiting for him, angry with him. He thought about driving to Denver with Sarah. Maybe they would talk about things. He could hear her voice, her saying that she was surprised at his reaction, her saying that for the first time she was not a little bit afraid of him. But then maybe they just wouldn't talk at all. Just sitting side by side would be enough. He could smell the blood in the house. He knew he was freezing but he did not feel cold.

Gunther reminded himself to breathe as he heard White stomping off snow from his boots inside the front door.

"Sheriff?"

"I'm in here, Gilly." When the man came into the room, Gunther said, "You didn't tell me nobody was home. Cold in here."

White didn't say anything. He leaned against the jamb, as if to balance himself. The five-shot Smith & Wesson .38 seemed almost to dangle from his fingertips, then he pulled it back into a tight grip. His nails were dirty.

"What now?" White asked.

Gunther looked at him for a second. "Unfortunately, I have to drive my daughter to Denver. I hate driving in snow."

"She okay? Your daughter?"

"She's good."

"Pretty girl."

"Looks like her mother. Thank god."

"Long drive. Denver."

Gunther nodded. "Marty's here with the gas."

"Oh, yeah."

"Let's go get that tractor going, so you can get back to work. The snow is falling pretty good now." Gunther stepped toward him, but the man backed away. Gunther was looking for any opening, any chance at all to grab the man's arm and control his gun hand, to do something. He stepped outside, White behind him. The snow was falling hard. The world was still, quiet.

Marty cautiously approached the house. There was no cover. He was hard to make out through the snow. He came on, his pistol out, walking slowly forward in a nervous crouch.

Gunther moved wide left, hoping to give Marty space to take a shot if he needed to. Marty yelled for White to put down the weapon.

"Your deputy is kinda upset," White said.

"It's your gun," Gunther said. "He didn't expect to see a gun. You know guns have a way of making people nervous. Especially cops."

"He's never seen a gun before?"

The snow fell.

"It's just the way you're holding it. Makes him think you might want to use it. Maybe if you put it in your pocket."

"White, you drop that gun!" Marty shouted.

"I don't think so, Deputy." White's voice was barely audible.

The snow fell. The world was so silent, Gunther thought. He thought about the drive to Denver.

Gunther watched Marty, his clean, hairless face, what he could see of it, his fear near ready to turn to panic. He watched as the young man froze, feet apart, shoulders square. Marty would never be the same. This was what Gunther thought. He saw the boy in the man's face. The snow. The swirling snow. That was what he saw.

Finding Billy White Feather

Oliver Campbell had never met Billy White Feather. He had never heard the name. But the note tacked to his back door had him out on the reservation at nine on a raw Sunday morning. *Twin Appaloosa foals at Arapaho Ranch,* the note said. *To purchase, find Billy White Feather.* The note was signed, *Billy White Feather.* He'd stepped out to find the note and no sign of anyone. He looked at his dog on the seat next to him. The twelve-year-old Lab's big head hung over the edge of the seat.

"You're not much of a watchdog, Tuck," Oliver said. "You're supposed to let me know when somebody's in the yard."

The dog said nothing.

Oliver didn't want to make the drive all the way up to the reservation ranch just to find no one there, so he stopped at the flashing yellow traffic signal in Ethete. Ethete was a gas station/store and a flashing yellow light. He got out of his pickup and walked through the fresh spring snow and into the store. He stomped his feet on the mud-caked rubber mat. The young clerk didn't look up. Oliver moved through one of the narrow aisles to the back and poured himself a large cup of coffee. He picked up a packaged blueberry muffin on his way back and set it on the counter.

"Three dollars." The young woman yawned.

"Three dollars?" Oliver said in mock surprise.

"Okay, two fifty," the woman said, without a pause or interest.

He gave her three dollars. "I'm looking for Billy White Feather."

"Why?"

"He left me a note about a horse."

"No. I mean why are you looking here?"

"I think he lives here. On the reservation, I mean."

"Indians live on the reservation."

Oliver tore open his muffin and pinched off a bite, looked outside at the snow that was falling again. "Do you know Billy White Feather?"

"I do."

"But he's not an Indian?"

She nodded.

"His name is White Feather?"

"That's something you're going to have to talk to him about. He ain't no Arapaho and he ain't no Shoshone and he ain't no Crow and he ain't no Cheyenne. That's what I know."

"So, he might be Sioux."

"Ain't no Sioux or Blackfoot or Gros Ventre or Paiute neither."

"Okay."

"He's a tall, skinny white boy with blue eyes and a blond ponytail and he come up here a couple of years ago and started hanging around, acting like he was a full-blood or something."

Oliver sipped his coffee.

"He liked on Indian girls and dated a bunch of them. Bought them all doughnuts till they got fat and then ran out on them. Now he's in town liking on Mexican girls. That's what I hear."

"His note said there are some twin foals up at the ranch," Oliver said. "Heard anything about that?"

"I heard. It's big news. Twins. That means good luck."

"So, what's White Feather have to do with the horses?"

"I ain't got no idea. I don't care. Long as he don't come in here I got no problem with Billy whatever-his-name-is."

Oliver looked at her.

"Because it sure ain't no White Feather."

Oliver nodded. "Well, thanks for talking to me."

"Good luck."

The door opened and in with a shock of frigid air came Hiram Shakespeare. He was a big man with a soft voice that didn't quite fit him.

"Hiram," Oliver said.

"Hiya," Hiram said. "What are you doing up this way, brown man?"

"I came to see the twins."

"Word travels fast. Twins. Something, that. How'd you find out?"

"I got a note from somebody named Billy White Feather."

"You know him?"

"Never met him."

"Stay away from him, though. He's bad medicine."

"I'm gathering that." Oliver looked at his cup. "I'll buy you a cup of coffee if you take me up to see the foals."

"You drive."

"You bet," Oliver said.

"I hate driving in snow," Hiram said. "Can't see shit in the snow. Course, I can't see shit in the bright sunshine."

Hiram grabbed his extralarge tub of coffee and Oliver paid for it. They walked out into the wet falling snow and climbed into Oliver's truck. Tuck moved to the middle and sat, his head level with the humans.

Hiram rubbed the dog's head. "He's looking good."

"For an old guy," Oliver said.

"I wish somebody would say that about me."

"I'm saying."

Hiram looked through the back window into the bed of the truck. Oliver had thrown a bunch of cinder blocks in the back to keep the truck from fishtailing on ice. Hiram nodded, "That's good, them blocks." He then started to fiddle with the radio. He settled on a country station.

"You like that crap?" Oliver asked.

"It's country music," Hiram said. "Indians are country people." He sang along with the song. "So, how do you know Billy White Feather?"

"I don't know him. Never heard of him until today when I got the note saying to contact him about buying the foals. When were they born?"

"Last night. It's George Big Elk's mare."

"So, they don't belong to Billy White Feather."

Hiram laughed loudly. "Billy White Feather?"

"His note said that if I was interested in buying the foals, I should contact Billy White Feather."

"More like Billy White Man. He doesn't own the shirt he's wearing. If he's wearing a shirt."

"George's, eh? Did George know she was having twins?"

Hiram shook his head. "The mare looked plenty big, but not crazy big, you know? Nobody up here was going to pay for a scan. Nobody does that. You know how much them scans cost?"

Oliver nodded. He turned his defroster on high and used his glove to wipe the windshield. "You must breathe a lot or something."

"Indians breathe a third more than white people. A quarter more than black people."

"Why is that?"

"This is FBI air."

"FBI?"

Hiram laughed. "Full-blooded Indian."

"I wonder why that guy put that note on my door?"

"Bad medicine. I wonder how he knew about the foals. I heard tell that Danny Moss and Wilson O'Neil run him off the reservation a few weeks ago. Beat him up pretty good."

"I wonder if I've seen the guy without knowing who he was," Oliver said.

"You'd remember him, all right. He's a big guy with red hair and a big mustache."

Oliver took the turn onto a dirt road that had not been plowed. "Think we'll be okay on this road?" he asked.

Hiram shrugged. "Long as the tribe hasn't plowed it yet. Those guys come by and make everything impassable."

"County does the same thing. They can take a messy run and turn it into impassable in a few hours."

"Cut it twice and it's still too short. Probably go to the same classes."

"Have you seen the foals yet?"

Hiram shook his head. "I hear tell they're damn near the same size and pretty strong."

"That's unusual."

"I heard that. I haven't seen them. They say the mare's good, too. Vet came up and couldn't believe it."

"Who's the vet?"

"Sam Innis."

Oliver nodded.

The snow let up a bit.

Hiram was looking out the window at the Owl Creek hills. "My father wouldn't set foot in these mountains," he said. "Scared him. Said there were witches out here." Then he laughed.

"What's funny?" Oliver asked.

"That priest over at Saint whatever-it's-called asked me the other day if I believed in god. I looked him in the eye and said, 'Why the hell not?' Then I told him the question is, does he believe in me? He didn't like that. I don't think he liked me saying *hell* in church."

"What were you doing in the church?"

"I go in there for that communion wine. It's the only booze I get. My wife won't let me have beer or nothing."

"Mine, either."

"You're married? Who would marry you?"

"She's crazy," Oliver said.

Oliver pulled the truck into the yard of the ranch. There were several people standing outside the barn corral. The snow had stopped falling and the sun was even breaking through in the west. They got out and walked over to the huddle of men standing near the gate. Tuck stayed close to Oliver.

The foals, spindly-legged clichés, were standing next to their mother, a fat-rumped, well-blanketed Appaloosa. The two colts were identical, buckskin in color, with matching blazes. Like the sire, Oliver was told. Who could tell yet whether they would thrive, but they were standing.

"What was the birth like?" Oliver asked.

A fat man named Oscar threw his cigarette butt into the snow. "I knew it was happening at about nine last night. I called Innis and he drove up, got here about ten. Then it went real fast. Vet pulled the first one out, but it wasn't easy. Her head and hoof were showing. He said a bunch of stuff, talking-to-himself stuff. You know how he is. He reached his hands in there to untwist her leg and I heard him say, 'What the fuck.' I never heard Innis swear before. He said he couldn't believe it, but he felt another head. I couldn't believe it, either."

A couple of the men whistled even though they'd heard the story.

"Vet said there was another one and there he stands. He gave them some shots and left a couple of hours ago."

Oscar looked at Oliver. "What are you doing here?"

"I got a note about these guys."

"Sam Innis was here all night," Oscar said.

"The note was from Billy White Feather."

The men grew quiet.

"How do you know him?" one of the men asked.

"Never met him," Oliver said.

"Why is he leaving you notes?"

"I don't know."

"He's an asshole," Oscar said. "He owes Mary Willow two hundred dollars."

"For what?" Hiram asked.

"Something about a horse trailer. She paid him to rewire it, but I guess he skipped with the money. Asshole."

"So, nobody suspected twins," Oliver said.

"Naw," Oscar said.

George Big Elk, a Northern Cheyenne man, came out of the house and moved to the rail. He greeted Oliver. "News travels fast," he said.

"Around here," Oliver said.

"Looks like they're okay."

"They're beautiful. Has she thrown before?"

"Twice. Lost the first one. Almost lost her, too. It was a mess. I thought she was all torn up inside, but then she had a foal the next year."

Oliver looked at the mare. She was tall for an App, with great conformation. "The sire as pretty as she is?"

"You bet," George said. "Handsome. He's handsome."

"Billy White Feather offered to sell them to ol' Ollie," Hiram said.

"I wish that wasichu would come around here," George said.

The men laughed.

"Well, I can now say I've seen the twins," Oliver said. "I will see you men later. Hiram, do you need a ride back down to Ethete?"

"I'm all right. But if you want to come back later, I'll have some buffalo triplets to sell to you."

"Come on, Tuck."

It was snowing again when Oliver arrived home to find Lauren rearranging the furniture in the living room. The rug was rolled up and shoved to one side. She had put towels under the feet of the sofa so that she could slide it across the floor.

"You're going to hurt yourself," he said.

"I won't complain if you help me."

"Do you know what you're doing?"

"No."

"Well, okay then." He helped her move the sofa across the room and turn it. He stood away with her and looked at it. "What do you think?" he asked.

"Nope. Back where it was."

They pushed it back.

"So, where'd you run off to this morning?"

"Went to see twin foals up on the rez."

"That's cool."

"It was pretty cool. Big App mare, identical babies, mother and children doing well. A real beautiful scene."

"Somebody's going to die," she said.

"You got that right."

"Why are you such a pessimist?" she asked.

"Hey, I didn't say it, you did."

"I only said it because I knew you were thinking it."

"Seriously, though, I hope those babies make it. They looked strong."

"So, who called you?" She followed him into the kitchen.

Oliver grabbed a couple of mugs and poured coffee from the pot that was sitting out. "Got a note. Tacked to the back door when I came in from feeding. It was from Billy White Feather."

"Who the hell is Billy White Feather?"

"Some white boy with an Indian fetish, from what I gather. I'd never heard of him."

"So, why'd he leave you a note?"

"Beats me. It's pretty weird."

"While you're in town I want you to pick up a package waiting at the post office." Lauren sipped her coffee.

"Who said I'm going into town? I just got back. I've got work to do around here."

"Please? It's snowing. I hate driving in the snow."

"Everybody hates driving in the snow," he said.

"Pretty please?"

"I love it when you beg. I'm leaving Tuck here." He looked at the dog. "Be a watchdog. Watch."

"Hey, he's old."

"He's still employed." He gave the dog's head a rub.

The new post office was right beside the old post office. Oliver wondered if a post office needed an address. The only part of the old one that was still used was its parking lot. It wasn't that the new lot was ever crowded, but the lines of the spaces had been painted so close together that no one could fit a truck into one. Oliver walked inside and handed the slip to the clerk, a large woman with large hair named Pam.

"You don't look like a Lauren," Pam said, looking at the paper.

"Haircut."

He watched as she waded through the piles of boxes into the back. He looked at the bulletin board beside him and wondered when they'd quit putting wanted posters on the wall. Someone was missing a tabby cat. There were some shepherd-mix puppies free to a good home. And there was a sheet with tear-off numbers offering guitar lessons from one Billy White Feather. Oliver tore off one of the tabs.

Pam came back with the box. "Here it is, Lauren."

"Thank you, ma'am."

"Just sign right here."

"Pam, have you come across a Billy White Feather?"

"Jerk."

"You've met him."

"No. He came in here and caused a ruckus a while back while I was out to lunch. Drunk."

"You know his address?"

"Yeah, Ethete."

"Ethete? But he's a white guy."

"You get kicked by a horse? His name is White Feather."

"Folks up at Ethete say he's a white guy."

"Well, maybe he ain't Arapaho, but he's an Indian. Got a jet-black braid down to his narrow ass."

"Then you've seen him."

"I wish I would see him. After what he said to that Dwight girl."

"Duncan Dwight's daughter?"

"Yeah."

"What did he say?" Oliver asked.

"I can't repeat it. But Duncan Dwight will shoot him if he sees him. And I wouldn't blame him."

Oliver picked up the package. "Thanks, Pam."

"You have a nice day now. Barn journey, as the French say."

Behind the wheel of his truck, Oliver called the guitar-lesson number on his mobile phone. A recording informed him that the line was
not in service. Of course, he thought. He put the phone away and
stared ahead through his windshield at the old post office. He was
near laughing at himself, taken as he was by what seemed to be a
mystery. The irony was double-sided, as, on one hand, he really had
no interest in Billy White Feather, whether Indian or white, and, on
the other, he recognized that pursuing an answer here was the same
as falling for whatever con game this Billy White Feather was running around playing. But why had this guy left him a note? Why had
he been at his place?

Oliver felt uneasy and so he called Lauren.

"You get my package?"

"Yep." He didn't want to alarm her, but he had to ask. "Has anybody come by today?"

"No. Why?"

"Just asking. Keep an eye out."

"Ollie?"

"I'll be home directly."

Even though he was anxious about getting home, his next stop was
Duncan Dwight's office. He was an attorney and a cattle detective.
He'd done Oliver's will and living trust. He was a short man who
was comfortable with his size. He never rode a horse, but he was a
real cowboy.

Duncan was chatting with his receptionist when Oliver walked
in. "How do, Oliver. What brings you around?"

"Just came from the reservation. An App just dropped twins."

"Really?" He led the way into his office. "Come on in."

"All healthy so far," Oliver reported.

"Pretty cool."

"They're gorgeous. Born last night. And somebody tacked a note to my door telling me about it."

Oliver watched Duncan respond to his tone. "Okay, a note," Duncan said. "Why are you saying it like that?"

"A note from Billy White Feather."

Duncan pulled a cigar from the box on his desk, snipped off the end, and put it in his mouth. "Billy White Feather."

"You know him?" Oliver asked.

"Never met him."

Oliver walked over and looked at a wall of photos. Duncan posed with various people, maybe famous. There were a couple of pictures of Duncan standing with prized beef. "Do you know anything about him?"

"Heard some people talking about him. Nobody seems to like the guy very much, if at all."

"I heard he said something to your daughter."

"I heard that, too, but she says she never saw him." Duncan lit his cigar. "What are you after, Oliver?"

"You know the folks up on the rez say Billy White Feather is a white guy?"

Duncan blew out a cloud of smoke. "White Feather sounds awfully Indian to me. What's eating at you?"

"This guy left me a note about buying horses that weren't his to sell. Left the note tacked to my door. " He sighed, thought about Lauren at home, and said, "I'd better get home."

"Maybe Billy White Feather isn't Shoshone or Arapaho, but everybody described him as an Indian guy to me," Dwight said.

"What else did they say about him?"

"Great big guy."

"Fat?"

"I heard big. Could be he's fat."

"Woman up at Ethete described him as a skinny blond man to me."

Oliver and Duncan stared out the same window.

"Well, I gotta go," Oliver said.

"I'll ask around some," Duncan said.

Oliver nodded and left.

Oliver arrived home to find Lauren dragging a bag of fertilizer across the yard. He got out of the truck and picked it up for her. "You're going to hurt yourself," he said. "This shit is heavy."

"You can carry my shit any day, cowboy," she said.

"Where do you want it?"

"By the hydrangeas."

"And which ones might those be?"

Lauren pointed.

Oliver put down the bag.

"What was that phone call all about?" she asked. "You got me all nervous and scared."

"Sorry about that. It's just that I found out about the twins up on the reservation from a note left on our door. And I started worrying because someone had been on the place."

"Well, you got yourself another note." Lauren pulled a paper from her sweater pocket, handed it to him. "It's from Billy White Feather."

"He was here?"

"No, some woman brought it by."

"Indian woman?"

"White. Never saw her before, but she was wearing one of those pale blue uniforms from that fast-food place near the grocery store. What's it called?" She searched. "Tasty Freeze."

"What did she look like?"

"Twenty-five, maybe a little older. Thick body, but not fat. Blond hair. Bad makeup."

"Did she say her name?"

"No, but her name tag said *Billie* with an *i-e*."

"Very funny."

"I kid you not."

Oliver looked at the note. *Sorry about this morning. Beautiful twins, but not mine. Call me if you need a ranch hand.*

"You sure you don't know this guy?"

"Now I'm not so sure. Maybe from a while ago. Maybe he used a different name. I'm trying to remember if I know any tall, short, skinny, fat white Indians with black blond hair."

That night Oliver couldn't sleep. He pulled on some jeans and a sweatshirt and walked downstairs. Tuck raised his head from his bed when Oliver sat in the mudroom to put on his boots. He told the dog to stay and Tuck put his head back down. The snow had stopped and the clouds had blown clear, allowing the temperature to take a serious drop. He folded his arms over his chest and walked out into the pasture with his donkeys. They stirred at the bottom of the hill and plodded their way up, investigating, hoping for treats.

Oliver thought about the twin foals and hoped they would be all right. He then considered Billy White Feather or rather he tried to consider him, tried to imagine him. He wouldn't have cared at all, except that the notes that had been left on the door of his home. It irked him even now that a stranger had stood on his porch without his knowledge. He worried for Lauren. Then the fragility of it all, everything, became so apparent. Strangers always had access to one's home. He could not be there all the time. He decided to find a companion for Tuck.

The donkeys came and stood around him, became still and peaceful. One of them lay down. Perhaps they were asleep. Who could tell? Perhaps he was still asleep and only dreaming that he was standing out in a pasture. The cold air bit at him some more and he decided, dream or not, he'd go back inside.

The next morning, after feeding the horses, after fixing a near-downed section of fence, and after a light breakfast of yogurt and toast, Oliver drove into town to the Tasty Freeze. He arrived a little after eight to discover they opened at eight thirty. He sat in his truck with his dog and listened to the news and weather on the radio. It seemed winter was coming early and hard.

An old-model blue Buick 225 rolled in and parked in a spot on the far side of the lot beside the dumpsters. A man got out and walked toward the restaurant. Oliver got out and waved to him.

"We'll be open in about twenty minutes," the man said.

"Does Billie work here?" Oliver asked.

"Who wants to know?" The man was rightly suspicious.

"My name is Oliver Campbell. Billie brought a note by my place yesterday and I just want to ask her about it."

The man looked Oliver up and down. "What kind of note?"

"It was a note about some horses. She delivered it to my place for Billy White Feather."

"Fuck Billy White Feather. If you're a friend of his, then you ain't no friend of mine." The man started to move away.

"I've never even seen Billy White Feather. I just want to know why I'm getting these notes."

"Yeah, well, that guy's got problems."

"You know him then," Oliver said.

"He came around here about three months ago messing with every waitress he could talk to."

"White guy?"

"Hispanic, I think. Anyway, that's what the girls told me."

"You never saw him?"

"I wish I had."

Oliver nodded. "Does Billie work today?"

"She should be here soon."

"Mind if I wait?"

"Suit yourself."

Oliver returned to his truck.

Another man arrived by bicycle. A tall, skinny, older woman parked her late-sixties Cadillac Coupe de Ville beside the Buick. A stout young woman with blond hair was dropped off by a man in a white dually pickup.

Oliver got out of his truck and called to her. "Excuse me, ma'am. Are you Billie?"

The woman looked at Oliver and then at the door of the Tasty Freeze as if she was considering running. When he was closer he could see that her name tag did indeed read *Billie*.

"It's okay," Oliver said. "I just want to ask you a couple of questions. You left a note with my wife yesterday. The note from Billy White Feather."

The woman's face showed some kind of relief, but she was still uncomfortable. "And?" she said.

"I just wanted to ask you about Billy White Feather."

"I delivered that note for my idiot roommate. I don't even know Billy White Feather."

"Your roommate."

"Yes, my roommate."

"And where might I find your roommate?" Oliver asked. He felt suddenly exhausted and perhaps overwhelmed. He certainly had no idea what he was doing in the parking lot of the Tasty Freeze.

"Not here," she said.

"You think I can drop by and see her?"

"Not here meaning not in town. She's gone. She's on her way to Denver to meet up with that guy."

"Billy White Feather."

"Yeah."

"Listen, I'd really like to track down this guy. Did she give you a forwarding address or anything?"

"I can't tell you that. I don't know you."

"I understand." He looked at the sky. "But you've seen my place, my wife. You know I'm not some crazy killer."

"I don't know that."

"I'll give you ten dollars for the address."

"Listen, I'm late for work."

"Twenty dollars."

"You're not a crazy?"

"No ma'am."

She gave Oliver the address and walked on into the restaurant.

Oliver returned home to do his chores. It was time for his horses to
have their shots and so he waited for Sam Innis, the vet. Innis always
delivered the vaccine and left it to Oliver to administer the shots. He
drove in while Oliver was combing out his mare's tail.

"I've got the drugs," Innis said conspiratorially, stepping out of
his rig.

"Thanks."

"First one's free." Innis looked around, then at the sky. "Any animals need looking at?"

"Everybody is standing. Got time for coffee?"

"A quick cup sounds good." The vet followed Oliver across the
yard and into the house.

Innis sat at the table in the kitchen. Oliver pulled some mugs
from the cupboard and reached for the pot.

"Where's Lauren?"

"Food shopping."

"Shoot. The only reason I come all the way out here is to see her.
You can tell her I said that."

"I will."

Oliver poured the coffee.

Innis yawned. "Sorry. Late night."

"Out partying?"

"I wish. Some foals died up on the reservation."

"The twins?"

"Yup."

"Damn. What happened?"

"Beats me. Failure to thrive. They looked good, real good. I can't
believe both failed. Twins are difficult." Innis sipped his coffee. He
handled the information like someone used to death.

Oliver was shaken by what he'd just heard. "I can't believe it," he said. He sat at the table, too. "They looked good."

"I'm going to do autopsies on them, but nothing is going to turn up. It just happens."

Oliver looked out the window at Tuck sniffing at the vet's tires. "George must be pretty disappointed."

"I think he is, but who can tell with him."

They drank for a couple of minutes without talking.

"It's a tough thing, all right," Innis said. "Twins are a complicated business. Complicated."

"Yeah, I guess so."

"Well, gotta run."

"Thanks for bringing the meds over," Oliver said.

Oliver checked the tractor and the plow blade. He would apparently be needing them soon. The sky had become fat and gray. Like a city pigeon. That was how his father had described a snow sky. He'd told Lauren the news about the foals and her eyes had welled up, but she didn't cry. She'd seemed more worried about him. Then he'd started talking about Billy White Feather again. She hadn't laughed at him, but she did stare at him with concern. She'd watched him unfold and fold the piece of paper with the Denver address.

Now he walked into the house to find on the kitchen table a paper sack and a tall thermos bottle standing next to it. Lauren was sitting, drinking tea.

"What's this?" he asked.

"Some sandwiches, some cookies, some coffee." She looked him in the eye and offered a weak smile. "How long have we been married? That was a rhetorical question."

"I thought so."

"I know you, Oliver Campbell. Go to Denver. Figure this out. Otherwise you're going to drive me crazy."

"I thought I did that anyway."

"It's a long drive, so stop for the night in Laramie."

"You've got this all figured out."

"Pretty much."

"Well, bolt the doors. I'll put the twelve gauge by the bed."

"You're scaring me again. I won't need it."

"Humor me."

Lauren nodded.

"Want to ride with me?" he asked.

"And who's going to take care of this place?"

"Just what am I looking for?"

"Billy White Feather."

"And why?"

"Beats me."

Oliver started toward the stairs, stopped. "He came to our home, Lauren. Stood on our porch."

"I know."

The drive to Denver, though long, was a familiar one. He knew when he promised Lauren he would stop for the night that he would not. It was only two in the afternoon when he reached Laramie and with only three more hours of driving it made little sense to lay up for the better part of a day. He grabbed a hot dog at Dick's Dogs, a place he could never visit if he were with Lauren, then continued on. He reached Denver just about in the middle of rush hour.

Sitting in traffic turned out to be better for his thinking than the driving. He looked at the faces of the other drivers. Any one of them could have been Billy White Feather. He had decided that Billy White Feather was actually a middle-aged, wheelchair-bound Filipina. Or a tall black man with a disfiguring scar down the center of his face.

If he found the man, what was he going to say? "Hey, why are you leaving me notes?" Or maybe "Stay out of my yard." Being there felt suddenly stupid. He had half a mind to turn around and head back to Laramie for the night. But it was only half a mind, after all. The rest of his mind wanted to see what Billy White Feather looked like.

Was he a Native guy or was he white? Oliver knew he wouldn't be able to tell by looking. Maybe everybody had him wrong. Maybe he was an Indian, but he sure wasn't Arapaho or Shoshone. Maybe he was a white guy with dark skin and a ponytail, going around telling all the wasichus that he was an Indian. None of this thinking answered the question of what he was going to say if he found the man.

He got off the freeway and made his way through town. He found the street and the address. It was a dingy neighborhood, made dingier by the fact that it was dusk now. Oliver parked in front of the small white house. A couple of teenagers eyed him as they walked by. He decided that sitting in his truck like that might get him into trouble, so he got out and walked to the door.

No one answered his knock. He walked around back, feeling uncomfortable as his head passed windows. He expected a pit bull to come running at him at any moment. In the back was a poorly maintained rectangle of grass, one of those circular clothes drying racks, and a partially disassembled motorcycle under a cheap aluminum cover. He tripped a motion-activated yard light over the peeled-paint screen door. His hands were shaking, but once he realized it, they stopped. He knocked on the back door and still there was no response. He sat on the concrete steps and looked at the battered Honda bike. It was fast becoming dark now. He looked again at the door.

Oliver got up and went back to his truck. He found some paper, the back of something on the floor, and wrote a note. He walked around to the back of the house again. As he attempted to wedge his note between the screen door and the jamb, the back door opened. A woman in a dingy yellow terry cloth robe stood rubbing her eyes.

"Who the fuck are you?" she asked. She was tall and extremely skinny. Oliver thought she looked like a user of some kind of drug, but decided he didn't know enough to tell. She had small features set in a narrow face with a sharp nose that was pointed at Oliver.

"Is this where Billy White Feather lives?"

"It's where he's supposed to live soon," she said.

"I was leaving him a note. Are you his girlfriend?"

"I'm her roommate." She sniffed like she had a cold. "What do you want with Billy?"

"Billy left me a note at my place up in Wyoming," Oliver said.

"Yeah?"

"I don't know this Billy and I want to know why he left me a note."

"You drove all the way from Wyoming for that?"

When she said it, it did sound sort of crazy.

"I'm calling the cops if you don't leave," she said.

"Do you know Billy?"

"Suppose I do?"

"Is Billy White Feather white or Indian?"

"What kind of question is that? You'd better get away from here."

"He put a note on my door and I don't know him. I just want to know what he looks like. Tall? Short? What?"

"Fuck you," she said and slammed the door.

Oliver left the note wedged inside the screen. He walked back to his truck and fell in behind the wheel. The teenagers noticed him again and walked back in his direction. He heard a siren in the distance. Billy White Feather might or might not be coming back to this house, but it hardly mattered. Oliver had left a note. Oliver had been on his porch.

Liquid Glass

Harold Beaver leaned over the engine and shook his head. "I don't know about this," he said. "I just don't know." He played with a torque wrench, spinning it around on his fingertips. "What if you've got a leak from the cooling system into the oil? I think you might."

"I don't," Donnie St. Clair said. "This motor is perfect."

"Then why are we working on it?"

"There's no leak. I have an exhaust tick. Let's just do it."

"Okay, listen, I'm telling you one more time," Harold said. "I pour this liquid glass in there and there's no taking it out. If there's even a tiny leak, that's the end of this engine."

"Just do it."

Harold removed the radiator cap. He poured the sodium silicate into a beaker, about a quarter cup.

"That's all it takes?" Donnie said.

"Listen, I think this is a bad idea." Harold looked Donnie in the eye. "Just let me replace your head gasket."

"And how much will that cost me?"

"Four hundred fifty."

"Dollars?"

"Yes, dollars."

"Pour it in," Donnie said.

"No, you pour it in," Harold said. "You can do it and just remember what I told you."

"Pussy," Donnie said. He took the beaker and poured the liquid quickly into the radiator.

Harold reached in through the window, turned the key, and started the engine. He joined Donnie back at the engine. "When the engine hits two hundred degrees, I think things should start to happen."

"You mean that awful ticking will go away?"

"That's the theory. I usually use this stuff for a quick radiator fix. Just a spoonful then. And you know what else they use this stuff for?"

"What?"

"To disable cars. Pour it in the crankcase, run the engine, and no part of the machine can ever be used again. None of it."

Donnie stared at his truck. "Listen," he said. "No ticking. You did it. You're a fucking genius."

"No, I'm a pussy, like you said. You poured it in," Harold said. He slammed shut the hood.

"How much?" Donnie asked.

"A dollar fifty."

"You see, that's what I'm talking about. Four hundred and fifty dollars, my ass. I'll pay you tomorrow. I can drive it now?"

Harold nodded. "I've got a bad feeling."

"Relax. I told you there ain't no leak." Donnie got behind the wheel and closed the door. "See you tomorrow." He gunned the motor. "Beautiful," he said. He rolled out of the garage.

Harold watched him drive to the end of the gravel drive, then stop. The truck made no sound. He could see Donnie frantically turning the key again and again. Donnie got out, stood away from the vehicle, and looked at it. He put his hands on his head and looked at Harold.

"Guess there was a leak," Harold shouted.

Donnie walked back toward the garage. "What now?"

"There ain't no 'what now.'" Harold pulled a cigarette out of the pack in his shirt pocket. "Your truck has experienced what is known as a catastrophic event. It's shit now. It's dead. I told you what would happen if there was a leak. There was a leak and it happened."

Donnie sighed and looked back at his truck and then back at Harold. He scratched his head. "There's no fixing it at all?"

"I'd have to replace everything. Except the body and electrical system."

"So, I fucked my truck."

"Pretty much."

"You got something I can drive for the day?"

"Take the Duster," Harold said.

"That thing works?"

"Most of the time. There's no second gear."

"Thanks."

Later that day, Donnie came back with the Duster. "You know, that's not a bad little car." He stood at the garage door and looked at the bronze Silverado pickup in the bay. "Whose truck is this?"

"Keasey's."

"Never-easy-Keasey? He's back?"

"Yeah, he says San Francisco didn't work out for him. Says he didn't like it, anyway. Sounds like he was doing pretty good to me."

"Nice truck. What's wrong with it?"

"Just an oil change. Let me describe that to you. That's when you take the old oil out and put in new oil, thus saving wear and tear on the engine and prolonging said engine's life."

"Well, fuck you. So, how's Keasey looking?"

"Big as ever. Looks good. Got a wife." Harold finished tightening the new filter. "Nice-looking woman. Pregnant."

"And he brought them back here?" Donnie asked. "She from here?"

"Black girl."

"Black girls are okay. White girls, too." Donnie lit a cigarette. "Why'd he come back here?"

"I didn't ask."

"Remember when he got his nickname?"

"I remember."

"We were up by twenty points against those Casper boys. Keasey lost the ball, threw the ball to the wrong man, even tipped a ball into their basket until the game was tied with three seconds left."

"I remember," Harold said.

"So, Keasey shoots and the buzzer goes off and there's that ball going around and around the rim. Everybody was standing up, waiting. Keasey was already running back to the bench with his fist in the air. Then the ball just dropped through the net and everybody went crazy."

"I remember."

"Every game was like that. Everything he did was like that. He was about to lose a footrace and the two guys in front of him got tangled up with each other and fell down. He won."

"I know." Harold poured the last quart of oil into the crankcase.

"One lucky son of a bitch. Never-easy-Keasey." Donnie shook his head. "I came up with that nickname, you know?"

"Right."

"I did."

"He'll be coming by here to get his truck in a few minutes and you can remind him."

"I will." Donnie looked over at his dead truck. "So, what will you give me for that piece of shit?"

"Give you? You owe me a dollar fifty."

"The body must be worth something."

Harold looked at the vehicle and then at Donnie. "Fifty."

"Done."

"No, fifty and I'll get rid of it for you. I'm not paying a dime for that piece of junk."

A 1976 white Chevy Malibu pulled into the yard. A tall, lanky man with a long dark braid unfolded from the passenger side. He walked toward the bay. The Malibu drove off.

"Keasey," Harold greeted the man.

"All done?" Keasey asked.

"Yep."

Donnie nodded. "Remember me?"

Keasey stared at Donnie and then shook his head. "You do look a little bit familiar."

"St. Clair," Donnie said.

"Oh, yeah. Danny, right?"

"Donnie. You remember me, don't you? I'm the one that gave you your nickname."

"What nickname is that?"

Donnie let out a confused, awkward chuckle and glanced at Harold. "Never-easy-Keasey."

Keasey's face grew hard. He looked away from Donnie toward his truck. "I always hated that name. So, that was you? Well, fuck you."

Donnie took a deep breath. "I never knew it bothered you."

Keasey's face relaxed and he smiled. "I'm just fucking with you, dude."

Donnie laughed.

"How much I owe you?" Keasey asked Harold.

"Thirty."

"Good deal."

"So, tell me, Keasey," Donnie said. "What brings you back here?"

"I'm from here. My wife is having a baby and I want the kid born here, too. Why are you still here? That's my question."

Donnie shrugged. "I left for a while. Went to Iraq. I like here better than Iraq. It's quieter."

Keasey sneered. "Iraq is for pussies."

"Fuck you," Donnie said.

"Just messing with you again," Keasey said and laughed.

Donnie tried to laugh.

Keasey looked at Donnie for few seconds. "I'm looking for a job. You know anybody in town that's hiring?"

"They need some help up on a few of the ranches," Harold said. He slammed shut the hood on Keasey's truck.

"I don't do ranch work," Keasey said.

"What kind of work you want?" Harold asked.

"I ain't choosy. I can work a register, a storeroom. I can make deliveries. I've worked in kitchens."

"Can you do construction?" Harold asked. "There was a guy from

Riverton in here, said he needs a framer. He left a card on the wall.
He seemed all right. I heard he pays pretty good."

"No good with tools," Keasey said.

"What did you do in San Francisco?" Donnie asked.

"I was a model," Keasey said.

Harold leaned against the truck. "Say what?"

"I was a model," Keasey repeated.

"Yeah, right," Donnie said. "Modeling what?"

"I was a hand model."

"What's that?" Harold asked.

"You know. In ads for watches and rings there are hands. I have
good hands. I had good hands."

"Had?" Harold asked.

Keasey held up his left hand, all four fingers of his left hand.

"What happened to the middle guy?" Donnie asked.

"Chopped off," Keasey said.

"We can see that." Donnie lit a cigarette. "How did you lose the
damn thing? Flipping the wrong person the bird?"

"You want a soda?" Harold asked.

"What?"

"A soda, a drink. Donnie, you want one?"

"Yeah," Donnie said.

"Sure, I'll have a Dr Pepper," Keasey said.

"Wouldn't you like to be a pepper, too," Donnie sang.

Harold stepped over and used his key to open the soda machine.
"Tell us about the finger," he said. "What happened?"

"Lost it in a bet."

Harold and Donnie looked at each other.

"That happens," Donnie said.

"All the time," said Harold.

"Fuck both of you." Keasey took a long pull on his Dr Pepper. "I
bet a bunch of money on the Super Bowl. I didn't have the money.
Guy says he'll take a finger. What could I say?"

"Could have offered him a toe," Donnie said.

"He didn't want a fucking toe."

"I would have given him my little finger," Donnie said.

Keasey gave Donnie an exasperated look. "He wanted the middle one, all right? Only consolation is that when I think about it I remember I gave him the fucking bird finger."

"Not much consolation," Harold said.

"At least I got workers' comp out of it. Insurance, anyway."

"How much does a finger go for these days?" Harold asked.

"A nice piece of change," Keasey said. "Let's just leave it at that." Harold raised his orange soda. "To fingers."

They drank.

"Hey, you guys want to make a buck?" Keasey asked.

"Let you chop off our fingers?" Harold said and laughed.

"No, it's a hell of a lot easier than that. I need somebody to pick up something down at the bus station in Laramie. As you know, my wife is pregnant, so I can't go. I can't go nowhere."

"What is it?" Donnie asked.

"A box."

"I figured that much. How big is the box? Is it heavy? And, most importantly, what's in it?"

"It's not big or heavy and it's just got some personal stuff in it." Keasey finished his Dr Pepper.

"Why didn't you just have it mailed to you up here?" Harold asked.

"My idiot friend in San Francisco lost my address and thought Laramie would be just fine. He didn't how far away we are from Laramie. So, it's waiting at the station down there."

"Can't they send it up here?" Donnie asked. "That's a long-ass drive all the way down to Laramie."

"They won't. Say they need to see my identification."

"You must be able to do it online," Harold said. "You can do everything online now."

"Okay, okay," Keasey said. "It's not really a shipment. It's something I left down there in a locker."

Harold cleared his throat. "I can't leave work. I've got cars backed up through the weekend."

Keasey looked at Donnie. "What about you?"

"No wheels. I fried my engine."

"You can take my truck," Keasey said. "I'll pay you five hundred dollars. All you have to do is bring it back here."

"I need to know what it is," Donnie said.

"What a couple of pussies," Keasey said. "It's personal, I told you. You want to make five bills or not?"

Donnie looked at Harold. Harold turned and walked over to stand beneath an old Ford Ranchero on the lift.

"Five hundred dollars."

"Is it drugs?" Donnie asked.

"No drugs."

"Counterfeit money?"

Keasey laughed. "No counterfeit money. Just some personal items, mine and my wife's."

Donnie looked again toward Harold, but his friend was at least pretending to work on the Ranchero's transmission.

"Listen," Keasey said, "I got to go pick up some things from the market for my wife. You think this over and tell me your answer when I get back." He turned to Harold. "Here's your thirty." He held up three tens.

Harold walked over and took the money. "Thanks."

"Thank you," Keasey said. "I'll be back in a few," he said to Donnie. "You'll still be here?"

Donnie nodded. He stepped over and stood beside Harold while Keasey got into his truck and drove away.

Harold went back to work on the Ranchero.

"What do you think is in the box?" Donnie asked.

"I don't give a shit what's in the box."

"Aren't you curious?"

"Nope," Harold said.

"I am."

Harold laughed. "You're curious about five hundred dollars."

"Sure. Why not?" Donnie said.

"He's not going to let you look in the box anyway. Jesus. A bus station locker? Gotta be drugs."

"Doesn't have to be."

"What else could it be? His toothbrush collection?" Harold said. "Just name one thing it could be other than drugs. Hey, if you want to do it, do it. Don't look to me for permission."

"I don't need your fucking permission. Toothbrush collection?"

"I'm going to get back to work now. If you want to wait for Keasey in the office, you can. You can stretch out on the sofa, watch Oprah, and enjoy your last hours of freedom."

"What are you saying?"

Harold flipped the wrench in his hand. "I'm saying that there's drugs in that locker and if you're crazy enough to go get them, then I'll be sending you cookies in the mail for a few years. And for what? For five hundred dollars."

Donnie waved his hand, dismissing Harold's words. "What channel is Oprah on?"

The Ranchero was off the lift and parked in the yard. It was the dark side of dusk when the bronze Silverado crunched gravel and Keasey got out. Harold stepped away from the tool bench he'd been straightening. Donnie staggered, nap-drunk, from the office.

Keasey walked over to Donnie. "What did you decide? Want to take a little drive?"

"What's in the box?" Donnie said.

"Like I told you, just some personal stuff," Keasey said.

"Any drugs?" Donnie asked.

Keasey made a show of trying to think, scratched his chin. "Nope, no drugs in the box. I would remember something like that."

"A grand," Donnie said. "I'll do it for a thousand dollars."

"Ain't this some shit?" Keasey said.

"It's a long drive," Donnie said.

Keasey gave Donnie a long, hard look. He glanced over at Harold, then back at Donnie. "That's a lot of money."

Donnie raised an eyebrow and stared back at the taller man. "It's not all that much."

"Okay, a thousand dollars." Keasey laughed. He looked at Harold. "Your boy here drives a hard bargain."

Harold nodded. "You guys mind discussing your business somewhere else? I've got to clean up so I can go home."

"Right." Keasey looked at Donnie and signaled with his head for him to follow. "Come on, tough guy."

Harold watched at they stepped away to the far side of Keasey's truck. He pulled down the garage doors while they talked. They shook hands. Donnie sat behind the wheel of the Silverado and Keasey sat in the passenger seat. They talked for a few minutes more and then rolled away.

Harold was asleep in his bed in his house on his street when someone woke him banging on his door. His girlfriend, Shannon, was beside him and made no sign of moving to get up. He looked out and saw Donnie on his kitchen stoop. Harold opened the door and looked at him, then at the sky just becoming light behind him. "What the fuck are you doing here?"

"I drove down to Laramie and picked up Keasey's box," Donnie said. He looked back at the big pickup parked behind Harold's Duster.

"Drugs. I told you."

"Are you going to let me in?"

"It's not even morning yet."

"Harold?"

"Come on in."

Shannon was tying her robe in the doorway as Donnie stepped into the kitchen. "What's going on?" she asked.

"Hey, Shannon," Donnie said.

"Go on back to bed, baby," Harold said.

"Everything okay?" she asked.

"Everything is fine. Now get some sleep."

"Okay," she said. "Night, Donnie. Don't be long, Harold."

"Everything is not fine," Donnie said once Shannon was gone. "Not fine at fucking all."

"Drugs, right?"

Donnie looked into Harold's eyes. "No drugs."

"You looked in the box?"

"I tried not to, but I got this feeling somebody was following me."

"You saw headlights?" Harold asked.

"No, but I got this feeling. I stopped at the rest area outside town and looked inside. I needed to know if it was drugs. It's not drugs."

"What the fuck is it?"

"Come with me," Donnie said. "You got a flashlight?"

Harold grabbed a flashlight from a drawer and followed Donnie out across the yard to the back of the truck. There was a regular-looking cardboard box sitting in the bed.

Donnie lowered the tailgate and pulled the box to the edge. "Look in there," he said. "Take a peek in there."

Harold opened the flaps of the box and looked inside, saw nothing, then remembered his light. He directed the beam into the box and saw a plastic bag but little else.

"Look close," Donnie said.

Harold did. "Is that a head?"

"It's a fucking head," Donnie said. He started to pace on the driveway. "Why is there a head in that box? It was on the seat next to me. I just drove two hundred fifty miles with a head on the seat next to me. Harold, that's a head, somebody's fucking head."

"Well, it's not drugs."

"I wish it was drugs."

"What I am I going to do?" Donnie asked.

"I guess you give it to the guy who paid you to pick it up."

"You don't think I should go to the cops?" Donnie sat on the tail-gate and looked up at the sky.

Harold sat beside him. "That's going to be a long conversation." He looked at the box. "It's not like this guy can be helped now. I say you give it to Keasey and forget about it."

"See, that bothers me. Keasey has a head in a box. What's going to keep him from putting my head in a box? He's going to see that I opened the thing and then he's going to know that I know he's run-ning around chopping off people's heads. Where does that leave me?"

"Then maybe you should go to the cops," Harold said.

"You're right about that conversation. I don't even know if this is fucking Keasey's truck. It might be the dead guy's truck for all I know. And I'm the one with his head, driving his truck. I tell them I went down there to pick up a package for a guy for a thousand dol-lars. What do you think will be their first question?"

"What did you think was going to be in the box?"

"What?" Donnie said.

"That would be their first question," Harold said. "What did you think would be in the box?"

"Yeah, right, and what do I tell them?"

Harold yawned.

"Sorry to fucking bore you," Donnie snapped.

"It's the middle of the night."

"It's morning," Donnie said. "It's morning and I've got a goddamn head in a box."

"Let's tape it up," Harold said. "Then you take it to Keasey and everything will be good."

"You're no help," Donnie said. He pushed the box back into the bed and shut the gate. "Listen, sorry I got you out of bed. Think about me while you're banging Shannon in there. Think about your old friend Donnie driving around in a pyscho's truck with a severed head in a box."

"What do you want me to say?" Harold asked. "I don't know what you should do."

Donnie got in and started the engine. He didn't say anything else, just drove off into the morning.

Harold was dressed for work and sitting at the kitchen table when Shannon walked in.

"So, what was that all about?" she asked. "Is Donnie all right? He looked like shit."

"Donnie's Donnie. Believe me, you don't want to know what's going on with him. Sorry he woke you up."

"I'll go back to bed. Wanna come?"

"Don't tempt me," Harold said. "Work, work, work, work, work."

"Well, don't forget to eat some lunch."

"Yes, Mother."

On his way to the garage, Harold spotted a white Malibu in his rearview mirror. It came up on him fast and rode his bumper. He couldn't make out who it was through the tinted windshield. The driver of the Chevy flashed his lights and blew his horn. Harold pulled into the parking lot of the Tasty Freeze. He got out of his Duster. Keasey got out of the Malibu.

"What's the problem?" Harold asked.

"Hey, where's your friend?" Keasey asked. He leaned forward, his posture combative.

"How the fuck should I know? I'm on my way to work." Harold turned back to his car.

"I'm talking to you," Keasey said.

"Give me a break, man. You made some arrangement with Donnie. I ain't his father, his brother, or his guardian." Harold reached for the door handle.

Keasey grabbed Harold's arm.

Harold didn't like that and he liked Keasey's attitude even less. He pulled back and punched Keasey hard in his left side. The man buckled, held on to the rear fender of the Duster.

"I told you to leave me the fuck alone."

"Donnie never showed up with my shit."

"Not my problem," Harold said.

"He's still got my truck," Keasey said, not yet fully erect.

"Again, not my problem."

Keasey still held his arm against his side. "Sorry I came on so strong." He seemed suddenly a completely different person. "Did Donnie get in touch with you? Call you?"

"I'm going to work."

"He didn't look in the box, did he?"

Harold wasn't listening, but he heard. He got behind the wheel and closed his door, started the engine, and left Keasey standing there. In his mirror, Keasey looked like a much smaller man. More, he looked scared, really scared. And this made Harold scared.

Harold pulled into his parking spot at the garage and felt his fingers clench the steering wheel more tightly. His mouth went dry. The hairs on the back of his neck stood up. Keasey's bronze Silverado was parked behind the garage. Harold was terrified and angry in turns. He got out and walked to the pickup. The bed was empty. Donnie was nowhere to be seen. Harold called his name. He walked around the building, ending up at the door to his office. It was still locked.

Inside, everything appeared in order, just as he'd left it, just as it had looked every morning for the past eight years. He dreaded Keasey coming and finding his truck at his place. He walked into the work bays and rolled open the big doors. He then went back to the Silverado. The bed was empty. The doors were locked. Harold could see inside. There was no box. At least there was no box. Harold told himself that if Donnie survived this mess, he would kill him.

Business went as usual that day. In fact, business was pretty good. People picked up their vehicles, paid in full, and left. Others dropped off their cars and trucks and left without complaint. And not a word from Donnie or Keasey. Still, Keasey's truck was parked behind the garage.

Harold called Shannon at home and asked her if Donnie had called or come by. He had not. He didn't have a number for Keasey. He thought about calling the cops and telling them the truck had been left there, but decided that he would sound like a nut or, worse, like somebody trying to cover his ass.

It came time to close up the shop and the truck was still there. He wouldn't worry about it tonight. He did hope that Donnie was all right, at least alive. He'd just locked the door connecting his office to the service area when he heard a noise. He unlocked the door and looked into the garage. With the big doors down it was pretty dark in there. He reached to the wall beside him and flipped the switch. Nothing happened. He grabbed the flashlight from the bracket by the door. He shined the light past the Land Cruiser in the middle bay and onto the back wall. Nothing. Another sound came from behind him in the office. He tried the light in there as well, but it didn't come on. He thought he saw someone pass by the window. He got scared. He went to his desk, opened his drawer, and took out his .38. He checked the chamber and saw it was loaded. He picked up the phone and called the cops on speed dial.

"Can you send a car to Harold's Garage, over on Cypress? I think I have an intruder."

Harold heard a louder noise from outside, like an empty fuel can falling over. He let himself out the office door. He could see better outside and so he turned off his flashlight. He walked along the wall of the building. He added a new fear to his current one, that the police would show up and shoot the man with the gun. He made his way to the back and the Silverado. He looked around.

It might have been there the whole time and he hadn't seen it. Regardless, it was there now. The cardboard box was sitting on an oil drum set against the wall of the garage. Suddenly it was hard for him to see, as if the darkness had fallen extra fast. He switched on his light and looked all around.

He looked at the box and stepped closer to it. He opened the flaps and peered inside. He shone the light into the box and could just make out the mass of light brown, maybe blond hair and maybe an eye. The box stank.

And now the police were on the way. His head was swimming. Fucking Donnie, was all he could think. Then he heard footfalls on the gravel around the corner. He hadn't heard a car, so he didn't think it was the cops. But if it was and he had the pistol up, they might shoot him. They would shoot him. He saw no beams of flashlights approaching the corner and so he thought it probably wasn't the police. He was shaking. He looked at the head, trying to figure out what to do.

When he looked up again he saw someone large. Larger than either Donnie or Keasey, but something wasn't quite right. He shined his light at the figure. The man was wearing a muddy suit, but above the collar of the filthy jacket was nothing. His once-white shirt was red and black, but there was no head.

Harold felt like he wanted to pass out. Was this a joke? The man, the body, was huge, six feet without the head. Harold looked at the box, picked it up, and pushed it toward the suit.

"I take it this is yours."

The muddy hands reached out and took the box, and the body walked away into the darkness.

When the police arrived, they found Harold sitting with his back against the front tire of the Silverado.

"Sorry, boys, it was a false alarm. The power went off and I'm afraid I got spooked."

The cops looked around. "Are you all right?" one of them asked.

"Yeah."

"Well, your lights are back on," the other said.

"Okay," Harold said.

"Sir, are you sure you're all right?"

"I'm sure." Harold stood and nodded.

The police left. Harold went back into his office. He switched off the light in the service area and locked the door. His hands were shaking. He walked over to his desk and was about to put away his pistol, but thought better of it. He put the gun in his pocket.

He sat on the sofa and switched on the television. Somewhere on the West Coast somebody was playing baseball. The daylight was startling even on the screen. Harold knew he would never see Donnie again. He knew also that Keasey was gone, along with his pregnant wife. The Silverado? He'd have to figure out what to do with that. He'd claim it was abandoned, maybe. Then he stopped thinking about all of those things, realizing that he was trying to distract himself. What had he just seen? What would he tell Shannon? Would he tell Shannon anything? Would he show up for work the next day? He looked back at the game. It was so sunny in California.

Graham Greene

I had done some work on the reservation nearly ten years earlier, helping to engineer an irrigation ditch that brought water from a dammed high creek down to the pastures of Arapaho Ranch. I slept on a half dozen different sofas during the seven months of the project. The tribe paid me well and I left, thought that was the end of it. Then just a few weeks ago I received a letter from a woman named Roberta Cloud. I was not so much surprised by the call as I was by the fact that she was still alive. She'd actually had a friend write for her as she was blind now, the letter stated. The friend said that Roberta needed my help. It was a short letter, to the point, without many details. The letter ended with an overly formal "Until I see you I am sincerely, Roberta Cloud."

I made the drive up from Fort Collins on a Thursday. I left in the morning and stopped at Dick's Dogs in Laramie for an ill-advised early lunch. I loved the dogs, but they never loved me back. I drove into a stiff early-winter wind that caused my Jeep to burn more gas than usual. The high-profile, flat-faced vehicle felt like it was on its heels as I pressed into the breeze. I hit Lander midafternoon and drove straight through to Ethete. Ethete was just a gas station with a convenience store. There was a yellow light at the intersection that flashed yellow in all four directions. I stopped and grabbed myself a cup of coffee.

A heavyset woman rang up my drink and the packaged cake I'd put on the counter.

"Think it will snow?" I asked.

"Eventually," she said.

I nodded. "Can you tell me how to get to Roberta Cloud's house?"

"She's on Seventeen Mile Road."

"Where on the road? Closer to here or Riverton?"

"Did you know it ain't seventeen miles, that road?"

"How long is it?"

"Changes," she said. "I've never measured it myself. Some people say it's only thirteen miles. Dewey St. Clair said it's nineteen, but I think he just said that because he was always late for work."

"How will I know Roberta's house?"

"She's at the first bend. There's a purple propane tank in the yard. Big one."

"Thanks."

I drove back to Seventeen Mile Road and turned east. After a couple of miles I saw the bend and there was the big purple tank. Someone had scrawled *Indian Country* across it in white paint, but the last letter of the first word and the last two of the second were worn off, so it read *India Count.* I rolled into the yard and waited behind the wheel for a few minutes. A black dog came trotting from the house next door. I got out and opened the back of my Jeep. I placed a carton of cigarettes on a stack of three new dish-towels and a twenty-dollar bill on top of that. The dog walked me to the door.

I knocked lightly. I didn't remember Roberta all that well. I re-called only that she was the oldest person I had ever talked to. She looked to be ninety back then. The gift was customary. I didn't know if she smoked, but the tobacco was important. I knocked harder and a woman called for me to enter. I did.

Roberta Cloud sat in a rocker across the room, backlit by the sun through a window. She didn't rock.

"Ms. Cloud?"

"Yes?"

"It's Jack Keene."

"Mr. Keene, you came."

"Yes ma'am. You call, I come. That's the way it works."

"I could get used to that," she said.

"I have a few things for you," I told her.

"Thank you, Mr. Keene." She pointed to the table.

I put down the towels, cigarettes, and money. "Please, call me Jack."

"Sit down, Jack."

I sat on the sofa under the window. The sun came through the glass and hit my neck.

"I was wondering if you got my letter," she said.

"You didn't give a phone number and I knew I could get here faster than the mail."

"And here you are."

"Here I am. What can I do to help you?"

"I want you to find my son."

"Ma'am?"

"My son. I'm one hundred and two years old. I'm going to die and I want to see my son one last time. I haven't seen him in a bunch of years, maybe thirty."

"Ms. Cloud, I'm not a detective."

"He's a good boy. I was twenty when I had him and he never gave me any trouble."

I did the math. "Ms. Cloud, that would make your son eighty-two years old."

"I reckon that's right."

In my head I did more math. I was told once that the average Native American man lives to be forty-four. I wasn't sure I believed the statistic, it being so shocking and sad, but I was certain it wasn't a gross exaggeration. Ms. Cloud's son would be defying the odds if he were still alive.

"So, you're telling me you haven't seen your son since he was fifty-two years old."

"His name is Davy."

"Do you know where I should look for David?"

"Davy. His name is Davy. That's what's on his birth paper. His name is Davy."

"Davy." I looked at Roberta Cloud's wrinkled face, her cloudy eyes. I wondered if she could see at all.

"When I met you years ago I knew you were a good man," she said. "And here you are."

"I'm glad you think that," I said.

"That's why I wrote to you."

I didn't know whether to feel flattered or like a sucker. "Ma'am, I have to say that I don't think I'm the person to try to find Davy."

She nodded. "You'll find him. I believe with all my heart that you will find him."

"Why do you believe that, ma'am?"

"Let's just say I have a good feeling about you." And then she let out a high little laugh that seemed incongruous.

"I see."

"The last I heard he was working in the restaurant in Lander. The restaurant would be a good place to start."

"There are many restaurants in Lander, Ms. Cloud. Do you know the name of the restaurant?"

"No, I don't." She reached over to the table beside her rocker and picked up a photograph. She pretended to look at it and then pushed it toward me.

"Ms. Cloud, eighty-two is kind of old to be working in a restaurant. Working anywhere."

"Here's a picture of Davy."

I took the photo and looked at it. I looked at the olive-skinned man with a long braid. He looked familiar. The man in the picture looked to be in his midforties. "It's an old picture, Ms. Cloud. Do you think I'll be able to recognize him?"

"You'll know him when you see him," she said.

I wanted to ask her if she was sure he was still alive, but thought better of it.

"What's his birthdate?" I asked.

"The second of December," she said quickly.

"The year?"

She directed her useless eyes at the ceiling. "I don't know," she said. Maybe she was crying.

"Ms. Cloud," I started.

"Mr. Keene," she said, her voice softer than before. "I'm going to die in one week. I can't stop it, that's the way it is. I know you will find my Davy."

There was nothing for me to say. Actually, there were many things I could have said, but none of them to Roberta Cloud. But I said the one thing that I could say to her and that was "Yes ma'am."

"Well, you had better hurry, Mr. Keene. The clock's ticking." She laughed.

Needless to say, I did not. Hurry, that is. What was I supposed to hurry up and do? I rose, bid her good-bye, and walked out into the cold March air. I looked at the propane tank and was sorry it had been so easy to spot. I stood just outside the door and heard no movement from inside. I wondered briefly what had prompted me to respond to the old woman's letter. Briefly, because I answered the question in short order. I was there because I was a stupid do-gooder, a typical idiot with a slight messianic complex. I thought I'd come up here and the old woman would ask for something simple, like a repair on the aforementioned propane tank, and I would do it, feel good about myself, and help out an old woman. I got what I deserved for being a nice guy.

I climbed into my car and drove to the reservation office. Maybe this would be simple. Perhaps Davy Cloud, if he was still alive, which I doubted, was living only miles away on the reservation. As I parked and got out I peered up to see that the sun was giving in to a sky that looked like snow. Inside, I found a lone woman sitting at a desk behind a long, high counter.

"What can I do you for?" she asked.

"A man could hear that a couple of ways," I said.

"A man could," she said. "But a man won't."

"Fair enough." I put the photograph on the counter. "I'm looking for this man."

"I'd be looking for him, too," the woman said. "He's a looker."

I nodded. "But he's about eighty now."

"Oh."

"His name is Davy Cloud."

"No Davy Cloud," she said. "There's a Roberta Cloud. No Davy Cloud."

"He's Roberta's son."

The woman looked at me with a sidelong glance for a second. Then she might have shaken her head. I wasn't sure.

"Could you check?"

"Check what?"

"Don't you have a register or a roll or something?"

"Yes, we have a list of everyone in the tribe. Is he Arapaho?"

"He's Roberta Cloud's son."

"Okay, I'll look up Roberta." She walked to a desk and sat at it, facing a computer screen. "We just digitized what we have. Here's Roberta. No mention of a son. But that wouldn't be that strange. Eighty years ago some people just had their kids and that was it. No paperwork, no nothing."

"A reservation phonebook?"

She came back to the counter, reached under it, and pushed the thin volume that was the phonebook toward me. "Look for yourself. One Cloud. Roberta Cloud."

"I believe you," I said. "Do you have any old phonebooks?"

"No."

"Is there a library on the reservation?"

She shook her head. "There's a library in Lander."

"Thank you. Sorry to come in with such strange questions."

"Every week some wasichu comes in here looking for an Indian nobody knows."

She was joking, but she had used Lakota slang for a white person and it kind of rankled me. "I'm not white," I said.

"You're not Indian," she said.

"True enough. Have a good day, ma'am."

I drove to the library in town. It was late in a steel-gray afternoon. I asked the cliché of a librarian at the reference desk if they had old phonebooks. They had some for Lander and a few for the reservation. Apparently the reservation hadn't started keeping a phonebook until seven years earlier. Still, I looked through all of them. I had nothing better to do with my time.

I found a computer, got online, and found a couple of David Clouds. Not one was Native. All were young and none were in Wyoming. And as usual I felt a little sullied by having been online.

I drove to a diner and tried to find some food. It should have been easy, given that I was in a restaurant, but it was not. The chicken soup tasted like soap and the club sandwich's only memorable attribute was that it was enormous. The waitress was an older woman who seemed well aware that the food was substandard.

"I would ask you if everything's okay," she said and left it at that, just filled my mug with coffee and walked away.

When she came back, I asked her how long she'd worked there.

"Twenty years," she said.

"That's a long time," I said.

"You bet your sweet ass that's a long time. Now every week feels like twenty years."

"Sorry," I said. "You ever have any Arapaho men work in the kitchen?"

"A couple. A Sioux guy worked the kitchen last year."

I showed her the photograph. "You ever see him?"

She studied the image. She gave it a good, very long look. "Nope, never seen him."

"That picture was taken about thirty years ago," I said.

She turned her head to the side like a dog and said, "There is something familiar about him."

"So, maybe he worked here?" I asked.

"What's his name?"

"Davy Cloud."

She shook her head, but said, "He does look familiar. But all Indians look alike to me."

"Well, okay then."

"No, he hasn't worked here since I've been here. I know that much."

"Thank you."

"Sure thing."

"Can I ask you something?"

"Shoot," she said.

"Is this chicken soup?"

She glanced quickly back at the window. "That's what I'm told. It's bad, right?"

"Tastes like soap."

"It tastes exactly like Palmolive dish soap. Exactly like it." She smiled at me as if we were sharing some important knowledge.

"Why didn't you mention this when I ordered it?"

She shrugged.

I put the photo back in my breast pocket.

I walked into two other restaurants, for no reason except that I had time to kill and didn't know what else to do, showed the photo, and got strange looks. When it was getting late I wandered into a run-down tavern with pool tables and a jukebox and ordered a beer. I said hello to the woman who was working the bar. A couple of bikers shot a game behind me. I thought, what the hell, and pulled out the photograph.

"Excuse me, miss, but have you ever seen this man?" I asked the bartender.

"What are you?" she asked.

"What do you mean?"

"Are you a cop?" At the word *cop* I heard the pool game stop briefly. "You some kind of private eye?"

"No, I'm an engineer."

That didn't help clear things up at all, so I decided to change my story. I told the next person that Davy Cloud had come into an inheritance. The heavyset blond young man with two sleeves of tattoos showed great interest.

"Is there a finder's fee?"

"No, I'm afraid not."

"Then why are you looking?" he asked.

"Friend of the family."

"Fuck that." He went back to playing pool.

"Let me see that picture," a woman said.

I did.

"I know that guy."

"You do?" She was about twenty and wouldn't even have been born when the picture was taken.

"Yeah, that's that Indian actor. What his name?" She bumped her forehead with her fist a couple of times. "Damn it. Sherry, come over here."

Sherry did, along with three leathery bikers. They all looked at the picture together.

The first woman said, "What's that guy's name? He was in that movie with Hal Kilmer."

"Val Kilmer," Sherry corrected her. She thought, gently pounding her own forehead with her palm. "Graham Greene. He was in that *Dances with Wolves.*"

"Val Kilmer wasn't in that," a biker said.

"The movie was *Thunderheart,*" Sherry said. "I know my movies. Yeah, that's Graham Greene."

I looked at the picture. I'd seen both of the movies and he did look a little like Graham Greene. In fact, he looked a lot like Graham Greene. Then I felt like an asshole for thinking that maybe the two men looked alike, as if it was because they were both Indians.

One of the bikers stared at me. He had a cliché red bandanna tied over his hair. "You know this guy?" he said, more an accusation than a question.

"Trying to find him for a friend."

"Why?"

"Some inheritance thing," the first guy I'd talked to said as he was taking his shot at the table.

"How much?" the biker asked.

"I don't know. The guy in the picture is about eighty years old now."

"Eighty? What the fuck does an eighty-year-old need with an inheritance?" The biker let loose a high-pitched laugh and his friends laughed with him.

I shrugged and took the photo back from Sherry.

"Thanks," I said.

"You're welcome," the biker said, not sincerely.

"That's Graham Greene," Sherry called to me when I was at the door. "I'm telling you that's Graham Greene."

After a night in a motel I returned to the library the next morning and looked at images of Graham Greene. The man in my photograph did look a lot like Graham Greene, but also different. Regardless, I didn't know where to look next. I decided to try the sheriff's office.

The inside of the office was as nondescript as the outside and in fact so was the sheriff. He was a new sheriff, though he was over fifty. I could tell because his clothes were so neat and crisp. His dispatcher was out sick and so he was manning the desk, he told me. I showed him the photograph.

"Looks like that actor," he said.

"I know."

"What's his name?"

"Graham Greene."

"No, that's not it. He was on that Chuck Norris television show." He scratched his head as he looked out the window. "Floyd something. Westerman. Floyd Westerman."

"This man's name is Davy Cloud. He's Arapaho and he's about eighty now."

"Why do you want him?"

"I promised his hundred-year-old mother I'd find him."

"You're shittin' me."

"I wish I were." I tapped the picture. "I can't find out anything about him. I was thinking maybe he has a driver's license."

"And you thought you could just wander into the police station and have somebody look that up on a computer, right?"

I blew out a breath, feeling pretty stupid.

"Well, let's take a look," he said. He laughed.

"Really?"

"Why not?" The sheriff used the computer on the counter. "What's the name?"

"Davy Cloud."

"David Cloud," he said.

"Davy," I repeated. "It was made clear to me that the name is Davy, not David."

"Doesn't matter," he said. "No Clouds at all."

"Okay, thanks, Sheriff."

"What are you going to do?" he asked.

"Beats me." I looked at him for a second. "What would you do?"

"You got a birthdate for Davy Cloud?"

"Day, month, but no year."

The sheriff snorted out a laugh. "Then I'd give up."

"You would?"

"I would."

"Thanks, Sheriff."

I liked the sheriff's advice. It made complete sense to me and I would probably follow it because there was nothing more I knew to do. I could not drag my carcass all over Wyoming looking for someone who was probably really a carcass. But before admitting defeat I decided to go ask around on the reservation one more time. I felt guilty because my search was really half-assed. That was due to my complete incompetence and also a sheer lack of any fundamentally important information. All I had was an old photograph, and for all I knew the man in it was an actor.

I parked in front of the little store at the flashing light. It was just starting to snow. I walked inside and grabbed a cup of coffee and walked up to the register. The same heavyset woman stood behind the counter.

"Remember me?" I asked.

"You were in here asking about Roberta Cloud."

"That's right. I found her. Thanks to you. Tell me, do you know Ms. Cloud?" I sipped my coffee.

"She used to come in more, but I haven't seen her in a long time. Why were you looking for her?"

"Wants me to find her son."

"Her son?"

"He's eighty-two years old."

The woman laughed.

"So, you don't know him."

"I didn't even know she had a son."

"Here's his picture. It was taken forty years ago, I think." I handed her the photograph.

"Never seen him."

"He doesn't look familiar to you?"

She shook her head.

"Like an actor?"

She studied the picture again. "Nope."

It pleased me that she didn't think he looked like anyone else. I put Davy Cloud back in my pocket. "My name's Jack."

"Delores."

"Delores, after Roberta, tell me who is the oldest person on the reservation?"

Delores looked at her feet and then out at the snow that was falling now in earnest. "It's going to be a mess," she said. "I'd guess that it would be Regina Shakespeare. I don't know how old she is, but she's almost as old as Roberta."

"Where is her house?"

"Last I heard she was living over on Yellow Calf Road."

"Where's that?"

"Off Seventeen Mile before Plunkett. Plunkett is where the tribal office is."

"Okay. How will I know her house?" I asked.

"Never been there."

"Thanks, Delores."

"Can I ask you a question?" Delores looked at my eyes. "Why are you doing all this?"

"I don't know. An old lady asked me to do something for her and I said I'd try."

"You could have said no," she said.

"I suppose I could have. But I didn't and here I am."

"You must have hurt somebody along the way, I guess."

"Excuse me?"

"You must be guilty about something."

I stared at her for a long few seconds. "Who isn't?"

I found my way to Yellow Calf Road. There were two houses on the dirt lane and they faced each other. On the porch of one lay a big black dog, a Doberman mix perhaps. The dog raised his head as I got out of my car and so I made the reasonable choice of trying the other house first. I walked through the deep yard and onto the narrow stoop. I knocked. I heard grunts first and immediately came barking as five or six dogs ranging from medium to huge came tearing around the corner of the house. They lunged while I tried to remain calm and slowly walk away. They did not chase me all the way to my car, but rather disappeared much as they had appeared. I looked across the road at the Doberman mix. His head was down again. I noticed smoke coming from the chimney pipe.

I walked to the other house and stepped onto the porch. The dog looked up at me and then closed his eyes. I knocked. A young man came to the door. He might have been in his midtwenties. He had two long braids that fell over his shoulders.

"I'm looking for Regina Shakespeare," I said.

"What do you want with her?"

"It's a long story, but I just want to ask her about Davy Cloud."

"Who's Davy Cloud?" he asked.

"Roberta Cloud's son."

"I didn't know she had a son. And who are you?"

"My name is Jack Keene. I'm a friend of Roberta."

"You can come in, but it won't do any good to speak to my great-grandmother. She's got Alzheimer's."

"I'm sorry," I said.

"She's in and out."

I stepped into the house. An old-fashioned wide-stance wood-stove kept the place very warm.

"Gammy," the man called her.

The woman sat in an old wheelchair. She didn't look up.

"Gammy, this man wants to ask you a question." He looked at me. "Go ahead."

"Ma'am, sorry to bother you, but do you recall someone named Davy Cloud? He's Roberta Cloud's son."

"Roberta Cloud," Regina Shakespeare said, surprising her great-grandson. "Why, she's even older than me." She let out a strong, throaty laugh.

"Do you know anything about her son?" I asked. "He'd be about your age."

"Alder wood pops too much, don't you think?" she said. She held up her index finger and smiled at the man. "What's this?"

"It's your finger, Gammy."

"Alder wood pops," she said.

The young man looked at me.

"Thanks for your time," I said.

"Sorry."

The highway was nasty as I drove back to Lander. The temperature had dropped suddenly and every curve looked like black ice to me. The snow was falling heavily now. I made it to a motel and lay in bed and did nothing. It was only Friday night and I had exhausted every avenue I could think of. I wondered what I was supposed to do for a week and then I remembered that if I waited a week Roberta Cloud would be dead. At least, she had told me she would be. I would have to go to her house the next morning and tell her that I had failed, that there was no way I could track down Davy.

I fell asleep wanting to dream about finding Davy Cloud, but I didn't. I dreamed about an old girlfriend that I'd never loved. And so I woke up in a bad mood.

The world was buried in snow on Saturday morning. My car along with it. I raked the windshield clear and then chipped and scraped off the ice. My fingers were numb when I started my engine. I returned to my room and let the car run for a while. I wanted the heat in the car and I wasn't sure if I could even shift and steer with my hands as frozen as they were. I snapped on the television for a weather report and there was Graham Greene talking to Val Kilmer in *Thunderheart*. Greene's character was complaining about Kilmer's character having a vision.

I fell in behind a snowplow on the highway and though it was slow going I felt more confident about the safety of the road. But that was short-lived as the plow turned around at the reservation border and I was left to push through six inches of snow with my Subaru.

There were a couple of cars and a pickup parked at Roberta Cloud's house. I tramped through the snow to her door and knocked. A young woman answered.

"Are you Mr. Keene?" she asked before I could say anything.

"I am."

"Come in." There were two other women inside the house and a tall man who drank from a large travel mug.

"What's going on?" I asked.

"She's dying," the man said.

"She's been asking for you," the woman who met me at the door said. "Who are you?"

"A friend," I said.

"Let's go then," she said. She led me into the room where Roberta Cloud lay on the bed under quilts.

"He's here, Roberta," the woman said and left.

"Mr. Keene, you're back." He voice was so weak, so soft I could barely hear her from five feet away.

"Yes ma'am."

"I knew you would find my Davy. Davy, my Davy." Roberta Cloud reached out her hand. She was so weak that I thought I could feel her life slipping away.

I stepped close and took the old woman's hand. It felt like a baby bird. Her bones felt like nothing. I said nothing.

"Davy, my Davy," she whispered. "I've missed you so much. I love you."

I didn't make a sound. I rubbed the back of her little hand with my thumb.

"It's been too long," Roberta Cloud said. She said that several times until her voice just trailed off.

I watched her face. I felt her leave. I didn't even hear her last breath. She was just gone.

One of the women came in and I looked up at her. She left and I heard her tell the others that Roberta Cloud was no more. There was no crying. I let go of her hand and stood up. She looked peaceful. I toyed with the idea that I was partly responsible for that. I also felt terrible that I had lied to her. I told myself it was not exactly a lie. I had simply let her assume something. But of course I had lied.

I left the room and joined the others in the kitchen.

"So, who are you?" one of the women asked.

"Ms. Cloud asked me to come here and then asked me to find her son, her eighty-two-year-old son. I couldn't find him."

"That's because he died when he was a boy," the man said.

"Excuse me?"

"He would have been my great-uncle, I think," one of the women said. "Granduncle?"

I looked back at the bedroom.

"What did she say to you?" the woman from the door asked.

"She thought I was Davy," I said.

"And so you were," the man said. "So you were."

PERCIVAL EVERETT is Distinguished Professor of English at the University of Southern California. His most recent books include *James*; *Dr. No* (finalist for the NBCC Award for Fiction and winner of the PEN/ Jean Stein Book Award), *The Trees* (finalist for the Booker Prize and the PEN/Faulkner Award for Fiction), *Telephone* (finalist for the Pulitzer Prize), *So Much Blue*, *Erasure*, and *I Am Not Sidney Poitier*. He has received the NBCC Ivan Sandrof Life Achievement Award and the Windham Campbell Prize from Yale University. *American Fiction*, the feature film based on his novel *Erasure*, was released in 2023. He lives in Los Angeles with his wife, the writer Danzy Senna, and their children.

The text of *Half an Inch of Water* is set in Adobe Caslon Pro. Book design by Rachel Holscher. Composition by Bookmobile Design & Digital Publisher Services, Minneapolis, Minnesota. Manufactured by Bookmobile on acid-free, 100 percent postconsumer wastepaper.